# Tears Of The Weeping Deer

### Harlie Hargraves

## Also by Harlie Hargraves

Save Our King
The Mush
Tears Of The Weeping Deer

_**Ghostly Universe Series**_
Drink This Wicked Blood

*Being different is not something to be ashamed of.*
*Take pride in your unique self.*
*Kick ass!*

# Playlist

Paris, Texas - Lana Del Rey, SYML
Season Of The Witch - Lana Del Rey
willow - Taylor Swift
The Prophecy - Taylor Swift
mad woman - Taylor Swift
Take Me To Church - Hozier
Where We Started - Thomas Rhett, Katy Perry
Not the End of the World - Katy Perry
School Nights - Chappel Roan
Sober - Demi Lovato
Take Me Home - Jess Glynne
Bigger Person - Lauren Spencer Smith
God is a woman - Ariana Grande

# Content Warnings

This novel contains potentially triggering aspects such as:

Murder, nudity, death, explicit language, possession, cruel pranks, disturbing haunting, rituals, human sacrifice, demons, brief sexual assault scene (not rape), violence, intense bullying, physical and mental abuse, etc...

This is a paranormal horror novel not meant for audiences under 18. You have been warned!

# Tears Of The Weeping Deer

HARLIE HARGRAVES

# Part I

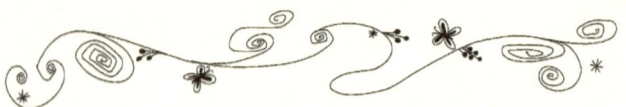

# 1. Swamp Hill

With every other passing second the dark green and pale-yellow legs of the rather interesting grasshopper adorned with tiny spikes twitch. Its golden eyes seem to follow her, but she knows they aren't. Just a trick of the mind is all.

By the looks of it the creature is holding on for dear life onto the seal of the truck window. The wind does its damn best to trample the poor thing, begging to rip it apart with rapid tugs.

For three hours it's been stuck with the traveling family. Headed along to their destination like an unexpected tagalong or perhaps it unwillingly hopped onto the truck. Like her, it was snatched away from its home and the other grasshoppers it may have known.

But an opportunity to escape this ridiculous move hasn't presented itself.

Maybe it's the fear of getting hurt that stops it from simply flying away. Too dangerous of a speeding wind. It might shed its thin wings. Not daring to let go until the old navy-blue Ford has come to a complete stop.

That of course hasn't happened yet, and she really needs to get to the lady's room. Her bladder keeps hinting at wanting to burst and ruin the old leather backseats. She's been crossing her legs for over thirty minutes now and the clock is ticking down to disaster.

How much longer till they reach Swamp Hill?

This is pure torture.

"Do you think there will be any boys who like wearing leather jackets and matte black nail polish?" The oddly pert voice of June Birkstone filters into the backseat and into her twin's ears. "There were a few at our other school. Maybe they're more country here? Yeah, this is gonna be good!"

With a roll of her eyes, July breaks her concentration off her little insect companion for just a moment.

She peers from the middle seat into the rearview mirror. Bland brown eyes that lack any sort of special luster reflect along with the faintly scratched lenses of her thick red framed glasses that sort of resemble swimming goggles. They pair poorly with the thickly cut brown bangs she gave herself to spite their drastic move.

It wasn't the best idea she's ever had.

She is never one to lash out. And yet the news of their sudden shift in life has snapped something within her. It was impossible then to stop herself from doing something stupid. Now she has to live with a terrible haircut while battling integrating into a new small-town school.

July never wanted to leave Dallas. It had so many places to escape to. Bookstores, libraries, and secluded parks that were perfect to slip away in. The food of course was unlike any other. The perfect tacos and best tasting coffee.

Why would she ever need to leave?

Oh, right. There is no easy way to forget it.

The father that was never around had mysteriously died and the lawyer discovered his mysterious manor was now in her and June's name. How convenient.

"I'm not sure. All you got to do is look." Their mother, Abigail as July likes to call her behind the older woman's back and to her face, sighs heavily. July watches her grip the leather covered steering wheel with a tight frown.

Hmm. It looks like she isn't the only one who's tired of June talking about boys. It's been like that since early this morning when they left. July still has no idea how much longer this trip will be.

This is getting old fast. She shouldn't have packed all of her books into a box.

The growing afternoon sun shines into the front wind-shield, illuminating Abigail's dark blonde curls that drip over her shoulders. A trait she shared with June. However, her hair is lighter in color and was recently cut to rest above her shoulders. They do have the same eyes. A stormy blue that boldens their many freckles. Sometimes they shine like diamonds in any sort of light.

It's almost cute. But it's something that sets them apart from July. Her hair is a dark muddy brown and so are her eyes.

For years she's assumed she took after their father. Of course, she hasn't been able to confirm such a theory. Abigail refused to show them any pictures of that man. She said he was no good and not worth their time. It only made July more curious.

She hopes to find some pictures of him in the house they will be arriving at soon, hopefully.

"What about you, July? Excited to meet new boys? I think they'd like you with that big brain of yours." It's sad how hard Abigail tries to include July.

Even she knows that not every conversation with June needs to have her in it. It just doesn't work that way. She never wanted it to.

July inhales softly before offering an uncontrollable grimace. That's not the answer she wanted to give. However, that is the one her mother gets.

Abigail shrugs before returning her attention to the older twin who adjusts the zipper of her pale pink tracksuit jacket. She obnoxiously pops the gum in her mouth and purposely smacks it. She does this to tease July knowing the icky sound messes with her eardrums.

June sends July a wink through the sun visor mirror as she notices her cringe in the backseat. Her stomach does a flip. Definitely not a pleasant feeling.

It's like her chest aches from the noise. Somehow it claws at her mind. She hates it. She really dislikes June right now. It never dips into a hate feeling.

So far nothing June has done has caused her to even think of that feeling.

July rips her attention away from those in the front seats to continue examining the grasshopper. It glides against the background of mighty cornfields waiting to be harvested. Lots of cows, goats, and the occasional donkey occupy bright green grass patches. She's even seen a few manmade ponds and timeless streams.

It's not hard to understand that Dallas is home to many different cultures and people but in the state of Texas it will forever be manned by those who farm and provide for themselves.

That she can envy. July craves to be able to do things on her own. But the cards she was delt with since birth have prohibited her from even getting her driver's license. She's eighteen damnit! Why can't her mother let her have one?

Oh, she knows why.

The perks of been the too sickly child.

The lesser twin compared to June. Just once would July like to prove them all wrong.

Abruptly, the grasshopper who's kept July company decides to hop off the window the moment the truck passes over the town limits. How fitting. The creature didn't want to come here either.

Abigail slows the truck down in case of pedestrians or possible cattle crossings. This gives her the perfect view of the welcome sign. It says:

*Welcome to Swamp Hill, Texas!*
*Where the corn is fresh, and the Southern folk are pleasant!*

By riding down the main road of Swamp Hill she's not sure if that's the case at all. This place is an utter ghost town.

Most of the shops are empty of Southern Folk. Literal tumbleweeds flutter across the streets from the strong wind that blows from the West. July wonders how the weather will be since they are now Southeast of Dallas and just twenty miles away from another small town called Swan Grove. She'd noticed that on the map she googled before losing temporary access to the internet.

Abigail trails the truck along slowly. June presses against the door to get a better look at the bare town. Her eyes widen as they approach a massive church right in the square.

July looks herself just in time to peak into the open doors of the rather crumbly building. It seems that almost all the town is inside. That makes sense. It's Sunday and church day too.

She jerks back abruptly as she accidentally makes bizarre eye contact with an elderly lady who steps outside with tears streaming down her face. Whatever was being said in there must have gotten the pale lady with stringy yellow hair wearing a frilly hat to sob like a newborn baby.

It's safe for her to say that she won't be part of that culture during her short stay in Swamp Hill. Because once she graduates in a few weeks she'll be gone and off to college. Perks of having more credits than required do come in handy to get out of this Hell hole early and far away from her sucker of a mother and attention whore of a sister.

Yeah, that's a good plan. She needs to keep her head down and stick to it.

July keeps her complaints to herself. Not wanting to upset Abigail more than she did this morning. She didn't mean to trip over the last few steps of their apartment building. It was an accident, again. It didn't result in any new bruising not brought on by June.

All thoughts and regrets from the last eighteen years of her life flee from her mind as they finally start to go down a loose gravel road that leads to their new home she's only ever heard about, Birkstone Manor.

As if a silent horn blasts to call upon something, a wave of dread floods her belly.

# 2. Birkstone Manor

Despite the town of Swamp Hill being surrounded by vast cornfields that look almost dead, the outskirts are one of the many gateways to the Pineywoods.

Perhaps they've been having a dry spell unlike most parts of the state. Which is slightly concerning. What if there is something wrong with this place other than it being in the middle of nowhere?

The rather enticing Pineywoods is made up of over ten different species of tree such as oaks and red ceder. Many of these massive trees entrap the gravel road the truck is paddling over. They create a tunnel of sorts that certainly gets denser the further along they are, making the pathetic wire fence surrounding the property disappear.

July peels back from the heated window. The branches reach out as far as they can. The trunk they're attached to is so hefty they have no choice but to lean towards travelers, scraping along the top of the truck itself.

She'd hate to be on this road during the night when the trees block the moonlight. Darkness would consume her in the blink of an eye and anyone else fated to be in the same theoretical position.

That's a nightmare she never wants to be a part of.

It isn't long before the woods let up and thin out to reveal the massive house at the end of the loose road.

Holy shit. She was expecting a house on the smaller side and practically falling apart. Certainly not this gigantic home. Their father really owned this along with his family for over a century. It's almost unbelievable.

July bites back a gasp. Jittery nerves swell in her chest at the enormous size of the place.

Her eyes squint at the sharp ray of sunlight that peers through the front windshield. It hits her right in the face. A burning blindness that fractures through the lenses of her glasses.

June squeals in disgust as Abigail pulls out of the woods and drives the truck into the oddly glamorous wraparound driveway. July rolls her eyes before getting a better look at the place.

She didn't think houses like this exist somewhere that's not hip California or fancy New York. But this house, being here in the middle of nowhere, is even more unsettling. It makes no sense. Her brain starts coming up with different reasons for it when the truck shifts into its parked position.

No one gets out. Silence engulfs the inside. July itches to get out and touch the glorious dark purple and black marbled posts that hold up the porch. There's over ten of them that she's sure surround the house.

The way the blazing sun hangs in the sky makes the outside of the deep brown manor glow like a lens glare of a camera. All of the stained-glass windows are brightened by the light as well.

July wonders what they must look like up close. She can't make out the image the windows are from all the way over here.

This curiosity is what influences her to get out of the truck first.

She inhales a deep breath that's full of strong ceder. It's rather refreshing. There's a good chance that the lack of floral pollen in the air will go easy on her allergies. She hadn't spotted any small fields of bluebonnets or Indian paintbrush flowers along the sides of the road.

Two more truck doors open and slam shut after her. July ignores June's complaints about the house. That's nothing new.

"I wouldn't be surprised if a big ass spider nest lives in this house. Like the big ass spiders from the one movie with the magic and wands." Sometimes her twin doesn't make a lick of sense. She really does act like a dumb blonde.

July rolls her eyes. "You mean *Harry Potter*."

June gives her a huff. Yeah, she already knows– thanks to her sister– that no one actually likes to be surrounded by nerds of any kind. Honestly, June can shove a hot poker stick so far up her–

"Oh, look. People." Abigail says in a light tone before moving in front of them.

That's when July also notices the old couple standing on the very last step of the porch.

Damn. Those aren't wood steps. They're made of the same marble as the posts. Upon further inspection she can see that the entire porch is made from the same stuff. Who the hell could afford to get those made? July doesn't want to know.

It's easy to see that these two old folks are married or at least together. They grip each other's hands so tightly that she can see their knuckles are whiter than a ghost. Their faces are utterly grim. She's seen sad people before but never someone so scared.

This is disturbing to say the least.

The urge to linger behind her mother and sister is overwhelming. July fails to fight it.

The woman wears a long black dress with billowy sleeves made from light blue lace. The color pairing doesn't illuminate her striking hair. Wavy strands of thin red flow down her back. She's got two simple pins keeping her hair out of her face. But it's the harsh frown on her face that encourages all those wrinkles.

July guesses she's seen things no normal person should. She pulls the sleeve of her shirt over her hands, not allowing herself to pick at the skin of her fingers. Instead, she bites the inside of her cheek.

The man on the other hand is much shorter than the woman. He's about July's height now that she's moved a few paces forward to get a better look at him. Curiosity swells within her, urging her to get closer and forget her own hesitation.

She can't stop herself from retreating at his appearance. He's got no teeth at all as he smiles wide to greet their mother. His wispy white hair blows in the sudden breeze.

It wraps around them. Almost yanking July to the ground. She plants her feet and braces herself around the wind. Various shades of yellow and brown leaves swarm the air as well.

She won't be falling over. Not yet anyways.

His worn black suit is paired with a blue tie the same shade as the lady's sleeves. Hmm. How fitting. They come as a pair.

The woman greets Abigail. "Hello. I'm Mindy and this is my husband, Larry. We've been caretakers of Birkstone Manor for more than thirty years. Welcome."

July cranes her neck to get another look at the house. It looks way older than thirty years. It's more than a hundred years old because of the way the dark red shutters have been nailed to the outside of the walls. Well, she did some research of the place before she and her sister were pulled out of school.

Why were they nailed back? That doesn't make sense. This place isn't that far from the Oklahoma border. She's sure surrounding towns get tormented with tornadoes and wicked rainstorms. A place like this should be able to hunker down in case of that and use the shutters to keep the windows intact.

Again, that doesn't seem right.

"Of course, we've spoken on the phone. Thank y'all so much for dusting the place before we arrived." Abigail doesn't smile too big when she catches sight of the inside through the large window of the front door.

July watches her mother's body shiver. She hopes it's not as atrocious as June's been fearing.

"Fuck this." June curses again and stomps up the steps and forces the husband and wife out of the way to get inside.

She can hear her shouts of displeasure from all the way over here. A truly mad woman. Well, that's no way to introduce yourself to those who literally cleaned the floor they plan to walk on.

The little things like that truly annoy July. Her sister should be grateful. Very little people get gifted an entire manor after their father dies.

After watching Mindy and Larry pull her mother aside to speak privately about house things July clears her throat, dislodging a potential sneeze before limping forward. It doesn't happen. She swallows the possibility of it.

There's no ache in her knee today which is good. She would be tortured if that were the case. These steps are so large. Their father must have been tall because this is close to being ridiculous.

As she pauses at the top step July pushes her glasses back up her nose. A bead of sweat drips down the side of her face. Maybe wearing long sleeves wasn't the best idea.

Spring is on the rise with it being the last few weeks of winter. This is just the first warm day they've had in a while, and it won't last long. She's got to enjoy it while she can before she's forced to be a mouth breather.

It will only get colder before the sun remains hot for the summer.

The inside is nothing like the wonderful aesthetic outside. Various animal-hide rugs dot the dark hardwood floors that shine. The smell of floor polish stings her nose. An intense aroma that hurridly clears the sinuses.

She spots many taxidermy animal heads hanging on the towering walls decorated with an antique looking wallpaper of a pale eggshell blue and different floral patterns. Large deer, small ducks, hogs, bears, and other creatures all staring down with empty eyes, naked of souls.

Yikes. July gulps down the bile that rose in her throat as she wanders into the living room. She's going to avoid looking at them for as long as she can.

A grand brick fireplace rests at the back wall. It hasn't been lit in years by the looks of the old ash. The small lanterns that hang from the visible roof rafters don't do this place justice. She tries to guess when the last time their bulbs were changed.

It's quite cozy despite the dead things and musty smell.

A small smile creeps on her face. Her heart skips a beat. This place could feel like home. She already feels somewhat comfortable here. It's far away from people and deep in the woods that no one would even try to visit.

Maybe she should bask in its dark atmosphere for the entire summer instead of immediately moving into the dorm of her chosen college due to her certain unwanted problems.

It's the perfect place for an introvert with too many medical problems.

She turns to voice her glee only to be disappointed by the gloomy expression that graces her mother's tired face.

"What is it?" She crosses her arms.

Abigail doesn't get the chance to answer as June hits her shoulder with one of the many bags in her hands when marching into the living room. She tosses them down before rushing up the spiral steps that lead to the other floor.

July hopes she's the one to trip on the way down and not her.

"Where's Mindy and Larry?" July grows concerned as their mothers shuts and locks the door before her.

Why aren't they staying like she assumed they would?

Abigail shakes her head. "Larry and Mindy said they won't be housekeeping anymore. The tragic death of Thatcher Birkstone has ruffled them so deeply. They're retiring."

It feels like the temperature dropped ten degrees here. She shivers, wrapping her arms around her thin waist.

Many questions swirl in her mind. Most won't ever be answered. But if she gets access to the local library or something close to one maybe she can figure out how their father died. Abigail won't tell them anything no matter how many times July's asked.

It can't be that terrible. Right? There's no way of knowing. If so, she truly hopes the couple weren't there to witness it. At least that gives the man some dignity.

June doesn't seem affected by this. She goes up and down the steps. The jumpy blonde discards her pink track jacket to reveal a tight white tank underneath, letting it drop to the floor.

"Will you stay still for once second, honey?" Abigail calls to June.

Reluctantly, her older twin does just this. Good. She can't handle her fighting before they have dinner.

"I'm bored. Let's go!" June declares and rushes over to grip July on the arm.

She never has the choice to say no. June doesn't take no for an answer anyway. Abigail encourages them to do something together occasionally. What she doesn't see is June ordering July around for her own pleasure.

And now she has no idea where they're going. The story of their lives. Listen to June and just maybe she won't smack July on the back of the head or giving her a wedgy when no one's looking.

Such a bitch.

Always the forced follower.

Never the one to take charge and make her own rules.

It just isn't supposed to work that way. She gets told what to do and June expects zero backtalk. It's safer that way unless she's begging to be humiliated.

"Be careful with her. I don't need to visit the nearest emergency room already!" The voice of their mother is far out of reach as they wind through the couches and recliners and coffee table of the living room to get to the kitchen.

July gulps down her fear. New places sometimes suck ass. However, it's the light grey walls and dim pink tiles of the floor that cause her to be terrified. The person who designed this place needs to give the original owners a much-needed refund.

Hell, it might not be a bad idea if they let June redecorate the entire house. At least it'll look more alive than dead.

The grip on her arm is tight. She won't be surprised if she wakes up tomorrow morning with bruises the shape of June's hand.

Suddenly and thankfully, June lets go the second her other hand touches the knob of the backdoor. July jerks to a stop and rubs her throbbing arm. Anger spikes in her but she douses it quickly with a flood of curiosity once her eyes land on the outside porch.

It really does line the entire house. This design is strange but not completely ugly.

Her footsteps echo on the marble steps as she tries to go after June who sprints through the cornfield.

July comes to a stop at the bottom step. Her eyes widen in shock.

This entire field should be dead along with the rest of the town. None of this is possible. And yet the entire thing is alive. Green stalks and bright yellow corn that's on the verge of needing to be harvested.

Maybe this part of the South has been getting rain. Perhaps just not every place benefit from it like this section of Swamp Hill. That doesn't sound right.

Damn. Even that suggestion fails to convince her. Well, she'll keep that to herself. She is by no means a plant expert or a meteorologist.

"Where'd you go, Sparky?" June's loud shout isn't what stalls her heart.

She collapses to the last step to grip her fast-beating heart, worried it might bust through her chest.

July can't recall the last time June called her that. A nick-name given to her for a specific reason of almost burning her finger off one Fourth of July weakened when they were little kids.

A very long time ago that's for damn sure.

# 3. Purple Door

This place is an all-consuming maze. There are twists and turns and winding curves that shouldn't be possible. Random stops that only further separate the twins.

July fails to keep up with June, the older sister by six minutes who continues to toy with her. She jumps out of random clusters of cornstalks to yank her hair. There is no chance to fight back before she disappears again only to come again to trip her.

That's one of June's favorite tricks. Stick out her foot when no one is looking and send July crashing down to have her face met with whatever surface she was once walking on.

She'd snicker. Have fits of disastrous laughs before managing to hoist her up before Abigail can catch June in the act.

How hilarious. How innocent of June to act so poised.

But this feels different. June shouldn't be this crazed. It makes her heart sputter each time she rounds another corner in the field. A pounding echo in her chest. The sun high in the sky shines down, pelting against the stubborn cold that pushes back with as much force.

And yet after a while July notices something worse than dripping sweat in the middle of a Southern winter. The silence. It isn't supposed to be this quiet. Where are the chirping birds and buzzing insects?

In a ditzy panic, she stalls her aching feet to gaze at the tall stalks that seem to cage her in.

Where did June go? It's been ages since she popped out in a rush to squeal in her ears like a raging goat.

After taking a deep breath July quickly pulls her long hair around her shoulder to braid it and tie it off with a band found on her wrist. The feel of the thick strands sticking to her neck from sweat is getting old. At least now she has one less thing to worry her about.

"June?" The name is muffled by the unexpected gust of chilled wind that sweeps through the corn, ruffling her bangs with its icy breath.

No response. Not even a cackle or snort. This is so not funny.

She sniffles. "Come out now, June. I've had enough of your games for one day."

There is nothing else to say. Her sister doesn't answer. July is sent into a panic.

Fear eats at her heart as she hurriedly begins to sprint through the horrid corn.

This is so unfair on so many levels. She hates doing what her dear sister wants. It's getting to the point where she just wants to scream. Maybe that isn't a bad idea right now. Abigail would hear and certainly come to her rescue.

But isn't that worse? Yes. Humiliation is worse than personal defeat. She's going to buck up and do this on her own. Like a fucking grownup.

In a flash the sky is covered with dark grey rain clouds. Well, isn't that something? Maybe they'll leak and provide ice cold rain.

The wind gets stronger the more July pushes through. She's given up on going along the jerky path and starts to cut through the corn like a hot butter knife.

The muscles in her arms and lungs ache from her vigorous movements.

This place never has an end. She'll be lost inside forever. There's no way out in sight.

Tears of fright slip down her face. Hiccups threaten to flood her throat. Her eyes blur with red anger. Why did June disappear?

Somehow her question is answered as a break in the corn is suddenly revealed to her. She could have sworn she had seen it sway in the opposite direction of the wind. Of course, that's not possible.

She's seeing things that aren't there or happening. A cruel joke her own mind plays on her. Another irritating addition to her fucked up view of herself.

July staggers out of the cluster of corn only to find herself in a perfectly cropped clearing the shape of a circle. Oh, that's fantastic. A crop circle. So far, she doesn't see any aliens waiting to abduct her. It's pathetic that she wishes little green men would come and take her away from this place.

Much to her puzzling relief the clearing isn't empty at all. On the contrary, she spots June closely examining a lone purple door in the middle of it.

"What the fuck is your problem today, June?" She curses as her limp jolts a pain up her thigh and hip.

A sore limb is the last thing she wanted. It's all her damn fault too. She should stick up for herself next time. There's always a next time with her sister.

June blatantly ignores her as she continues to trace a random branch over the door. It's a deep purple but not quite eggplant. The wood is very old with many marks and bruises. Various gashes litter the surface as well.

From what she can see it's got no hinges because it's not attached to any sort of frame.

She stalks forward with a firm frown set upon her face.

The door is standing perfectly straight. By the looks of it it's not even in the ground. She's got no idea how it's standing like this. Best not to find out either.

The clouds in the sky get darker, blocking out the bright sun completely, turning the sky an icky color. The wind soars, whipping around them.

July struggles to stay standing as June seems content in looking at the door.

"We should go. It's going to storm. June?" July pleads with her.

She says nothing. Damnit. June needs to answer her. Now isn't the time for this.

July clears her throat as another gust of chilled wind snakes around her body. Her flesh erupts in goosebumps. It seeps into her fragile bones, imprinting on her being. It's not like anything she's felt before. It's charged with energy that doesn't feel right.

They really need to get out of here.

Their mother's call snaps them both out of whatever entrapped them.

She watches June shake her head and drop the stick. Her pretty blue eyes are glazed over, pupils wide and filled with dangerous longing. For what? She has no idea.

Without thinking, she offers June her trembling hand. Her sister glances at it before shooting her a wicked smirk. Then she kicks up dirt to hit her in the face.

July stumbles back, wailing from the pain brought on by the dirt now filling her eyes.

So much for glasses being the convenient shield to this kind of torture.

Her sister's evil laughter echoes into her ears. July falls backward, her ass hitting the ground in a thudding heap.

"Damnit." She cries not only from the stinging sensation in her eyes but from the pity she feels for herself.

She could have tried fighting back at least this one time when Abigail couldn't see. Maybe then she could've found some higher ground and got much needed revenge. But of course, nothing ever works in her favor.

June always has the upper hand. That bitch.

After crying all she can of the dirt out of her eyes July sneaks a glance at the purple door. Just looking at it makes her shiver. There is no need for a random door out in the middle of a corn field. And yet the thought seems to trigger another thrust of breeze.

It shapes the corn to pull forward. The stalks reach out for something. For her.

July staggers onto her feet. Adrenaline pumps in her lively veins. She wastes no time hurrying back as far away from that thing as possible.

She finds Abigail waiting for her on the porch with a worried face. At least that's something familiar.

# 4. Strange
# Happenings

W ho knew pizza could be delivered so far out of town. The sweet old lady who owns Swamp Hill Pizzeria was happy to send her grandson out to bring them their best pizzas to try. Plus, they were the only place open after ten.

Free of charge of course.

July guessed it's because they're new to town and they want to show off. Not that any of them complained about free food. The pineapple bacon pizza that was dropped off on the front porch was her favorite.

Thinking about the caramelized fruit upon melty cheese now gets her stomach rumbling again. She can get a snack down from the kitchen later after sorting through these many boxes.

Abigail claimed that the manor is far too big for them to be separated. Too many rooms to keep track of. Especially on the second floor. Endless halls of empty spaces that could swallow July hole if they tried.

This of course meant the twins would be sharing a room. Now that wasn't what she wanted to hear as she shoved a thin slice of pizza into her mouth. At least June wasn't happy about it.

And yet she still found a way to make it worse with her annoying orders of how things should go in their new room.

That's why she makes sure all of her things are kept on the left side of the room. She's nearest to the big French windows. The stained glass is framed to resemble the cornfield. It's oddly fitting.

Most of them were made to picture the town. She recognized a few of them designed to look like places that she seen as they drove down the main road.

She's not sure why the original owner did that. Maybe to remind them that there's an outside world other than this lonely manor and field. July would want that at the back of her mind. A failsafe of sorts. A place to escape to when the times get truly revolting.

She neatly folds her underwear into little triangles and places them precisely into the dresser drawer. It's a pleasant pale wooden furnishment that pairs well with the twin bed frame made of the same material. Much different from the carefully designed iron daybed frame that June has.

They couldn't be more different. She hardly can find ways they're alike these days. She's glad about it too.

"Make sure none of your gloomy stuff gets on my side of the room. I don't want the darkness to ruin my glamour than it already has." June grips while brushing her hair with a silver brush in front of her fancy pale pink vanity she got for their birthday two years ago.

Her pretty pale blue nightgown glows in the lights lining the large mirror.

They turned sixteen. June got a makeup vanity. July got a gift card to the local hospital gift shop. That seemed fitting with all things considered in a strange way. July was a regular visitor on account of her clumsy accidents and brutal allergy flare ups. And of course, her various doctors wanted to make sure no new leaking holes appeared in her heart, forcing them to go back into her chest and patch her up.

Perhaps something that shouldn't be bragged about.

July nods her head after finishing buttoning up her sleep shirt the color of freshly mowed grass. She inwardly cringes at the large pale pink scar in the middle of her small chest.

She shoves the memory of waking up in the hospital after her second open heart surgery out of her mind before plopping onto her bed.

There are still many boxes to unpack. She's too tired to worry about it now.

July places her glasses onto the bedside table and shuts off the small lamp that emits a dim yellow light. The covers are heavy over her body and trap in her warmth.

Abigail mentioned that someone from town will be coming tomorrow to fix the heating system that failed to roar to life earlier. She made sure to find those extra blankets. Reluctantly, she gave a few to June before making up her bed.

Thankfully, the second her head hits the pillow she's out like a light.

Her sleep was rather peaceful while it lasted. She was faced with a pleasant dream of slipping through a crystal-clear pond in high snowy mountains. The water was warm and offered the best comfort.

She hated having to be torn away from it when June's loud snoring woke her.

Something always ruins her happiness.

June's snores are so profound that they echo out into the hallway.

Their mother suggested keeping their door open in case of an emergency. Now the only trouble she's suffering from is a growing headache.

She can't think of a time her sister ever snored. This is certainly new for her. She must be sleeping damn well to sound like a wailing hog. Yes. That's exactly what she sounds like.

July bites back a chuckle, afraid to disturb the slumbering beast.

It takes little effort to fetch the large Texas history textbook she left on the bedside table. She cowers with it under the comforter with a small flashlight.

Her sister never allowed a nightlight in the room. Claimed to need complete darkness to fully preserve her beauty sleep. Whatever that means.

So, this little light was her only safe option. She made sure to have a blanket thick enough to block the flash from pissing June off. That hasn't happened in a long time. The last time she accidentally woke her June tossed a lamp at her. It nearly tore her nose off.

July's been more careful about that.

The clock she had Abigail hang on the wall strikes midnight.

She yawns before flipping the book page. The paper is thin and cool to the touch. Its glossy finish only slightly reflects the light.

Suddenly, a chill rushes through her.

July peels out of the comforter, allowing some light to escape. She watches her heated breaths fan out in front of her face. Her brows squint in confusion.

The man on the radio weather station claimed they'd be getting a heat wave during the night. An early sign of spring. And yet she's shivering under three heavy blankets. This doesn't seem right.

The heating system must be really fucked then.

She begins to turn towards June. She halts as a chilling groan from deep in the hall slithers into the room.

*Buurrrrhhhhh.*

Her heart stutters, erratically skipping beats.

Not even a moment later is it followed by a sickening creak of wood. Oh, this is so much creepier.

*Creeeaaakkk. Crrrreeeaaakkk!*

It's like heavy yet precise footsteps. Where did that come from? Shit.

July jerks her gaze to June, silently hoping she got out of bed to find the bathroom without her knowing. Much to her horror June is dead asleep, now much deeper into slumber. Not even the sounds of her snores filter into the room anymore. Oh, crap.

More of the terrifying sounds go off in various places in the house. Some in the hall. Others right within the wall next to her. Like it's getting closer and closer to her, to their room.

There's no time to think about it. July shoves the blankets off her legs, drops the book and light, and gets her trembling hands onto June's shoulder. No matter how hard she shakes her sister the older girl won't wake. Her sleep-induced sounds keep flowing.

Nothing is going to wake her. July won't have anyone to save her from whatever the fuck is out there.

"Fuck." July hisses when the loudest of the creaking seems to be right at the very much open door.

She keeps still standing next to June. Her hands clench tight at her sides. Her chest heaves up in down with panicked breaths.

It's so dark she can't make out anything.

July rushes back to her bed after there's a shocking bang on the outside of the room.

Tears drip down her sore eyes. They're still throbbing after the dirt June kicked in them many hours earlier. She's wishing she had that spitfire now more than ever.

Her fingers barely grasp onto the flashlight when a disturbing smell leaks into the room, stinging her nose like a thousand little bees.

It's such an intense stench of rot. It spreads everywhere. She swears that it's wafting in a faint yellow cloud.

No. She must be sleeping.

This is a nightmare.

A bad dream that she can't fucking wake up from. She really wants to wake up now.

The smell is extremely strong. It causes her head to grow light which encourages her eyes to slink shut. July forces herself to keep up straight. And yet it's too much for her. The sounds. The smells. That awful feeling that's now pushing against the inside of her skull right at the very front.

She's the only one experiencing this. Neither June nor their mom is aware. Why her?

Not wanting to, July collapses on her back with the flashlight still in her limp hand.

Before whatever this is that's messing with her makes her fall asleep, she jerks the light, aiming towards the doorframe.

A small gasp escapes her as she peers at a dark shape with long twisting horns.

She tries to scream. It lodges in her throat. Tears file down her cheeks and slip over her chin.

July fails to shout as this force coaxes her to sleep, leaving her vulnerable, unable to stop it from doing her harm.

# 5. Girls Rule, July Drools

Strikingly bright sunlight instantly seeps into July's eyes when June pulls back the old dusty drapes of the windows.

She jolts awake. A migraine quickly settles in the front of her skull. It's a sickening pounding, a hammer bashing against her brain.

Of course it's followed by three harsh sneezes.

Before she can pitch off another June's shoving two pink allergy pills into her shaking hands.

Her sister's pale yet mesmerizing eyes are thin as she takes in the sight of a sweaty July. Perhaps three blankets were too many.

"Take these before you sneeze your brain out. I don't feel like getting Mom to come and pick up all the gooey pieces." She huffs and wraps a silky pink robe around her shoulders.

July watches her breath come out in a fog.

The room is rather chilly despite the sun that shines through the stained-glass windows. Many pretty colors such as red, green, and blue are scattered over the dark brown walls.

Despite the main part of the manor being decorated with that ridiculous wallpaper everywhere else is empty of it. Bare of anything dramatic. It's all so gloomy. She's deciding if she should welcome that darkness or be weary.

After last night–

Wait. What happened last night?

A memory so vivid– mostly fractured– zaps in her mind. Something about a chilling sound out in the hall and a figure in the doorframe.

With a starling gasp July jumps out of bed, the blankets pooling onto the freezing floor. The wood makes a creaking sound. The familiarity of it makes her wince.

July rushes to June who sits on her vanity stool putting large curlers into her hair. Her fingers clutch her sister's shoulder in a truly gripping hold. June jerks back, messing up the nude pink lipstick she was in the middle of applying.

She doesn't bother muttering an apology.

"Please tell me you heard all that last night. You must have." She gets down on her knees despite her hip protesting with a forceful throb.

June curses down at her. She hits her right on top of the head due to a familiar reflex.

July has no chance to block the hit. Her skull groans in protest. Damn, that's going to be there all day.

"I have no idea what you're talking about, freak. I slept perfectly. Now hurry and get dressed. I cannot be late to school because of your clumsy ass." June gives her a sinister smile before shoving her backwards.

She lands on her backside with a thud. Her lips reel back due to a hiss from pain.

Anger floods her body. The tears building in her eyes are hot and beg to fall.

July won't let them. Instead, she uses June's bed frame to hoist herself back up. It takes all the strength she possesses to get steady. Her chest aches slightly. Not a good way to start the day.

Where did she leave her inhaler? It must be down in the kitchen.

As June ignores her once more, she stripes off her wrinkled pajamas that are damp with night sweat. It's a salty stench she needs to get rid of.

She declares she'll be showering and will keep the door cracked in case something goes wrong.

Her sister mumbles whatever before waving her off.

She sniffles and gathers her clothes for the day, pressing them against herself to shield from the cool air and slowly heads out of the room and takes a crisp right, further down the hall.

It's darker here. The light from outside has no windows to seep through. Dust bunnies flutter in the newly disturbed air caused by her small footsteps. Halfway down the hall a slight breeze pushes around her.

July stops abruptly. Her chest pounds. She felt this before. The same as last night.

When a snap shouts to her right in a random locked room she quickly rushes into the massive bathroom before slamming the door behind her. She'd rather drown in the shower after slipping on the slick tile before being eaten or beaten by whatever is out there in the house.

July keeps her eyes wide open as she washes her hair with nice smelling shampoo. It's a pleasant rose scent. A soothing sensation that floods her nose. But not enough to distract her from the danger that lurks in Birkstone Manor.

And yet as she uses an expensive loofa made for those who are skin-sensitive to glide moisturizing body wash on herself she can't help but wonder if it was all a dream.

It would explain the odd night sweat. Maybe that's why June didn't hear or notice anything either.

Of course, it was all a really bad dream. She wasn't taunted by noises and didn't see anything dark standing at the entrance of their room.

She shoves those possibilities out of her mind and welcomes in the reasonable explanation.

A small smile filled with relief spreads across her pale face.

The buzzing isn't going to stop no matter how July begs it to in the silence of her own mind.

Voices of students and school faculty roam through the cafeteria.

She wishes she was back in the truck and heading straight to the manor. This is a mistake. Being here without knowing anyone or anything about this place is fucked up. She hates this more than when June shoved her out of the truck, doing her best to make sure she landed disastrously.

As her sister continues speaking with the vice principle, she gets a good look at what they're dealing with.

It's easy to make out the band kids with their obnoxiously large instrument cases and ugly green and red uniforms.

The token goths and emos lurk in the far corner. Their black makeup and clothes alone act like the night sky, refusing to let any stars shine through. And yet that's the point.

Don't be seen by anyone or forever be swallowed by the all-consuming flock of unoriginality.

She grips the strap of her backpack tightly, shifting on feet covered in dark brown Vans with lime green laces.

There's a ticking in her jaw. She pushes up her glasses that threaten to slip off her nose.

Her body stiffens as a thunderous ruckus sprawls out into the room. Unfortunately, the rowdy group in the middle must be all the jocks. Their shouts of laughter and hollers cause her guts to twist, pulling her insides like saltwater taffy.

She can smell their cheap cologne from here. Do they bathe in it before leaving the locker room? Seems like it.

July feels bad for those who had no choice but to sit around them. A few kids look upon the annoyingly echoey crowd in distaste before shoving their faces back into their books. Others roll their eyes and place headphones over their ears. Their music colliding with the voices of those who wear red and green letterman jackets.

However, panic rises in her chest. There's one group missing. Every school has them. The popular girls. The cheerleaders.

Damn demons from Hell is more like it.

June gazes ate the pack of wild boys. Their hoots clearly aimed at the new piece of meat dressed in a pale pink shirt and low rise bootcut jeans.

She curled her hair. The thick short strands bounce on her shoulders with the few steps forward she takes. However, her stride is stalled by a high-pitched squeal.

July jolts. She cringes at the group of girls dressed in cheer uniforms as they swarm her sister who can't help but beam at them.

But hey, at least she found the little devils she'll want to avoid the rest of her time here.

Reluctantly, she slides closer to her sister, wishing she was somewhere dark and alone.

One cheer leader with long pale blonde hair smiles brightly at June. "Hey, I'm Trudy. I'm the team captain. Me and the girls wanted to invite you to the team. We've heard so much about you and how you carried your old team through the football playoffs."

Another girl with deep dimples and bouncy brown hair nods firmly. Her thick ponytail decorated with a sparkly white bow swinging with the movements of her rather small head.

June opens her mouth to address these vulture-like girls only to suddenly remember she has a fraternal twin standing right behind her. Even just existing, July proves to be a thorn in someone's side.

Her eyes catch June's blue ones. All of a sudden, she wishes hers were like that too. Maybe then people would be nicer to her. Everything about her seems to invite unfriendly behavior. Most compare them to each other, discussing which is the better of them. June is the correct choice every time. She's learned to live with that fact. It doesn't mess with her like most may think.

Instinctively, July squares her shoulders in the opposite direction, hunching into herself. Maybe she can fold into herself enough to disappear. Yeah. That sounds like a nice idea.

"I forgot you were right there." June sneers low enough for her and the cheerleaders to hear.

She gulps down her hesitation. Forcing herself to bite the inside of her cheek to contain a retort. That'll only earn her a smack in the arm. A go-to-hit when they're surrounded by people.

Most of the time she'd rather take a hit than words. It somehow hurts less.

June's pink painted lips spread into a multilayered smile. The corners of her mouth too curled to insinuate kindness. The showing of her teeth of course telling her to keep quiet or else.

She doesn't want to find out what 'or else' might be. Not in front of all these new and uninviting faces.

"Why don't you run along. Find an abandoned classroom to squat in. And for the love of God, please stay away from me for the rest of the day." There's certainly a bite to her words.

She feels their eyes pinned on her. She won't meet their curious gazes. She's not going to give them any interest.

July nods her head softly. June's false smile morphs into a satisfied smirk.

This is humiliating. Walking away from them. From her. It's the same as before.

For the rest of the year everyone no matter who they once hung out with before will congregate around her. None will leave her side. They will listen closely to the rumors she will certainly spread, the lies she will conjure to cause trouble, and her orders of any degree.

They won't be able to see through her games. She's caused many breakups, fights, and outbursts at their old school.

July's afraid of what June might do now that they only have eight weeks left of school. And high school alone without this demon of a sister is already tough.

She's absolutely fucked.

# 6. Unexpected
# Company

Half the school day is gone and already talk has spread about her and June. She's not surprised about this of course. This was going to happen no matter what.

However, what she's struggled to figure out is if this talk originated from a random student or June herself.

Who opened their mouth and said that June isn't a natural blonde? July can't fathom who actually questioned her sister's oddly perfect tanned skin. Where are the tan lines or fake tan patches? Either someone who really doesn't want her sister to dominate all the cliques of this school or June herself. June would certainly do such a thing to derail potential rivals. To even the playing field just a smidge.

She'd rather not find out the true answer. It will just stress her out more than she already is. Already does it take everything in her not to pull out her own hair.

July lingers in the main hallway that all the senior homerooms occupy. A few stragglers rush past her, knocking on her shoulders like she isn't standing there, hurrying to claim a seat at the lunch table. A bunch of fucking heathens.

Her mouth curls in a snarl fueled by disgust.

There's no way she's going to face June so soon after this morning. She does not have a death wish over it. No need to embarrass herself more.

And yet what else is there to do?

July grips her backpack strap and fiddles with the end of her braided hair with her free hand.

The yellow hall lights flicker above her. Random clicking sounds from classroom clocks shout into the open air that is utterly filled with gross dust bunnies and all the germs cultivated from these nasty kids.

She moves down the hall slowly, peering into the rooms to figure out which one she'll occupy for the entirety of the lunch period. It's what she did at their old school. The teachers never cared. No one was missing her anyways.

And yet none are satisfactory. They all scream gloom and boredom.

At the very edge of the hall that leads to the main foyer and cafeteria, July gives a huff.

Her hefty green jacket that's lined with fleece suddenly feels stuffy. She peels off her backpack and momentarily struggles to remove the jacket from her shoulders and arms.

A small sweat breaks across her forehead. Shit. This is so pathetic.

She moves to wipe her flushed skin only to stop when noticing an older woman with rich brown hair and tiny glasses strut past her. In her arms is a stack of worn books. They scream old and wisdom. So many informative words must be scattered all over the withered ivory pages.

Gathering her things she limps forth, hoping to catch up with the woman.

"Excuse me? Where's the library? I'm new and haven't been able to find it yet." That's a lie.

She wasn't even looking for it till this very moment when the thought of books flooded her mind. Why didn't she think of it sooner?

The woman stops abruptly with a sharp hoot. The flowy velvet skirt she wears the color of forest green swishes around her legs. It looks nice paired with her black fitted top that has long sleeves that scrunch at her wrists.

Her light brown eyes seem to glow against her tan skin. A pleasant shade of honey hit just right by a ray of sunlight. Why isn't this woman in Dallas or Houston in a modeling agency?

"Well, I'm heading there now, darling. Care to join me?" Her Hispanic accent is very pleasant and oddly welcoming.

A familiar sound here in Texas. Something that usually hints towards fantastic food and wonderful company.

Of course, she rather be smothered by dusty books with the presence of this woman than all the rowdy kids who will surely finds ways to torment her upon June's permission.

Yeah, sounds fucking terrifying.

July gulps down her sudden jolts of nerves and nods her head fiercely, happy to have found someone who might share the same love of books she does.

"Excellent." The woman grins and continues with July hot on her trail.

They travel down the foyer and go through another hall at the far right. The lights are dimmer than all the others in this school. It creates a very cozy atmosphere. Especially as they stop in front of a set of double doors carved from dark red wood that leads to the library.

The woman gestures for her to go in first. Feeling safe enough to so do, July complies, her feet finding it easy to move forward.

The smell of old books and earthy scents from a large blazing candle resting on the librarian's desk flood her nose. She inhales deeply before picking a spot to sit at one of the tables that occupy the main space. All the shelves circle in the sitting area, creating a rather enclosed feel. One that she welcomes greatly.

To some it might seem suffocating. To her it's homey and a comforting shelter.

She sets her backpack down. July peels the zipper, opening the main compartment to retrieve the brown sack containing her mustard and ham sandwich and the current textbook she's been reading.

After laying them on the small black plastic table she watches the woman settle on the rolling chair behind the main desk.

"So, you're the librarian." It's obvious now. An older woman carrying books to the library. Well, maybe not that old. Perhaps around the same age as her mother.

An easy observation.

Even stupid people can conclude the same.

"You call me Ms. Tibbs like the rest of the bratty kids here." Her sharp dark eyebrow rises high.

July smirks. "My apologies, Ms. Tibbs. I'm new here. My name's July Birkstone."

She expects to receive a similar set of words. But the librarian, Ms. Tibbs, simply frowned slightly. It's not an unnoticeable gesture. And yet it's one that she moves to quickly correct with a soft smile.

Huh. That's strange. Maybe she's heard of the manor she and her family recently moved into.

Yes. That seems right. A reasonable explanation.

Her pale fingers grip the sides of her textbook. Her teeth fiddle with the inside bit of her cheek. Her wide eyes as she takes in the sight of Ms. Tibbs, examining the titles of her books.

The woman notices her curious stare.

"Yes?" She asks with a curt tone.

She shakes her head and fishes out her sandwich. "Nothing."

The librarian nods as well, stands tall with books in hand, and moves around the room to put them back where they belong.

Silence develops between them. Not an unpleasant type either. It's a nice change from the chaos that is high school.

Neither of the two speak anymore. They sit in this silence and simply enjoy it like the bookworms they are.

Ms. Tibbs is shelving the books. July is reading hers. The perfect match.

This must be the start of a great friendship. She can feel it in her bones.

# 7. Bedtime Nightmare

July's finger glides over the smooth page of her Texas wildlife book. The words of medicinal plants and dangerous plants to avoid start melting together. Her vision blurs as she attempts to move onto the following paragraph.

The hour is late. She really should stuff her small flashlight into the bedside table drawer and call it a night. And yet she must read on. There's so much more to learn.

There's a slight pain in her neck. She's been leaning too far underneath the sheets. Yet another sign of it being too late in the night for this.

A little clock that Abigail hung on the far-right wall of their room ticked at midnight almost thirty minutes ago. They have school in a few hours. She really must shut her eyes now.

Oh, but just maybe another paragraph or two. What's the harm in that?

Her eyes wander over the following pages. More like them fusing together in a fuzzy cloud.

Now this is quite interesting. The difference between poison ivy and poison oak–

*Creeaak.*

The light in her hand trembles. The heart in her chest clenches, alerting her nerves to flutter erratically.

July shakes her head. Nope. She didn't hear anything. It's all in her mind.

She gently clears her throat before continuing. What was she reading? Ahh, the difference between–

*Mmooopp....*

That's a different sound surely. Like a muffled burst. As if someone's popping bubble wrap underwater.

July pauses again, not daring to turn another one of the book pages. They shake between her fingers, threating to slice into her thin flesh.

With as much ease as she can muster, July slips the sheet off her head. Locks of her brown hair fall over her shoulders, draping across her dark blue night gown.

It's a hot night even though most of the state is still battling winter. She opted to wear this instead of a pair of pajama pants and a sweater.

But now she's regretting it.

A sudden chill sweeps into the room as she carefully lifts the flashlight. She aims at the open doorway of their room, guiding the light out into the hall as much as it can go.

Before she gets a chance to glance over the bold print of her book again another noise filters into the room from the hall.

That's no trick of her mind. Not this time. It wasn't that last time either. It couldn't have been.

This is not in her head. Fuck!

After taking exactly three deep breaths to stabilize her heart, July slowly gets out of bed.

The wood floor is cold under her feet. They haven't had a chance to go into town again in search of a rug. And they won't get one until June is certain it's the one she loves.

July walks towards the door in no rush. Before she reaches the hallway a loud shout shoots into her ears.

*Eeeeaaarkkkkk.*

*Eeeaaaaarkk.*

*Diiiieeeeee!*

July stumbles backward. Her back collides with the foot of her bed. She topples down on her knees.

Her mind pounds within her skull, aching from the noise and that last ridged word that shouldn't have been possible at all. No one else is awake besides her. But that isn't true, is it?

There's a ringing in her ears now. Her eyes water. It's hard to see where she's going. She barely manages to stand.

July moves to wake June only to stop abruptly upon seeing her sister thrash in her sleep. Her thin yet lean-muscled body convulses. Almost like she's having a seizure. Wait! This is a seizure.

Despite having extremely blurred vision and the worst migraine of her life July gets back on her knees and does her best to shake June's shoulder. Her chest quakes with fear and sudden determination to wake her suffering sister.

Sadly, the force she's using isn't strong enough, causing her to wait for whatever this is out. The fear she once felt for the frightening sounds has long gone out of her being. Now she's too distracted to be confronted by whatever it may be.

Within a small second later it all stops. Her headache. June's erratic movements. And the echoing noise disappears. All that's left is the harsh breathing coming from her.

She feels something warm leaking down the sides of her neck.

July gently touches her flushed skin and shines the light on her fingers. What she finds is startling. Bright red blood coats her hands. Her eardrums must have burst and suddenly healed like it was nothing.

What caused such a thing to occur? July fails to recall any natural disaster that can even attempt something like this.

She licks her dry lips and peers at the opening of their room. A whisper of something dark slips away before she can catch a better look. She's seen whatever it is before. She couldn't remember then but now she does. It having come back a second time refreshed that memory. July didn't know she didn't remember till now.

Something is in this house.

But it must wait. July is more concerned with June.

Her sister's pretty blonde browns unfurrow, releasing the crease between them. She snuggles her face back into her satin covered pillow. Those little snores fill the room once more.

Everything is back to normal.

July doesn't want to read anymore. This event has tired her out. She turns off the flashlight and puts it away.

She doesn't bother with cleaning her skin of fresh blood. A wave of drowsiness consumes her. The second her head hits the pillow her eyes shut tight.

# 8. Rot Away

School has been decent. July avoids June like the plague. June picks and chooses the best time to bully her. Which is either in the early morning on the way to school or during passing periods.

July has been tripped on numerous occasions. A few have caused her to skin her knees on the courtyard pavement and be sent to the nurse's office. Others were done by her sister's new friends. They're more like blind followers.

Damn. June's entire life is like a cult that she does her best to control. Most of the time it works. They do what she says. Never ask any questions. Always worshiping the literal ground she walks upon. A damn cult.

Today was slightly different. The morning went almost without any trouble. There were a few hateful words spewed from June's pink glossed lips but that was it.

Most avoided her due to an unknown reason. It didn't make any sense. But who is she to complain?

And as June put the large curlers in her hair before bed, she even glared at her. That's mild compared to the usual string of curses or July's personal favorite, 'you're an absolute waste of space' speech.

Perhaps she should be grateful nothing wild happened.

However, as she sits in bed with her arms crossed, a new range of possibilities flood her mind. June could be planning something big. Going quiet before a calculated outburst is familiar. A little tell that her sister has.

But somehow that doesn't feel right either. Maybe she just didn't have the energy to waste any words or hits on July today. It's rare and it does happen from time to time.

None of that matters now. The hour is late, and all the geometry work she had to catch up on today drained her. Her mental state is suffering for it.

She makes sure her dark brown sleep shirt is buttoned properly before snuggling underneath the blankets she piled on top of the comforter.

This night is chilly with little chance of her sweating in her sleep.

There are only a few hours till the sun starts to rise and she still isn't asleep. June has been snoring for a long while. She's in a deep sleep that July envies.

No matter how hard she clenches her eyes shut nothing happens. She just lays there with clamped eyes that fail to call upon the inky depths of sleep.

This is hopeless.

However, after listening closely to the wind swish against the outside of the manor her mind starts to grow silent. Her body uncurls gently. July's breathing evens out.

Ah. Finally, she's asleep. And yet something furious sinks into her nose. Waking her up from a very faint slumber with a rumbling start.

July squeezes her nose shut.

It's such an awful smell. A stench of spoiled uncooked eggs and perhaps soured soil from too much rain. The combination of both is truly cruel and so pungent.

She does her best to conceal a gag as she fetches her flashlight. The light fails to provide any real cause of this smell.

Her eyes water from frustration and irritation.

She shines it across the room over to June's little daybed.

Her sister tosses and turns madly. A slight pain enters her chest at the sight of this. She gulps down another gag before calling out to her. Hoping that she might wake up and escape whatever nightmare she's in.

Damn. Maybe this is July's nightmare. That gross scent is all in her head.

She considers the idea further but then dismisses it fully on account of June scrunching her nose and mumbling about July needing to shower more.

So, even in a ruined sleep June can smell it too. She's not sure how helpful that is. But at least her mind is more awake than she first thought. June will be alright.

July groans softly to herself. This smell isn't going away anytime soon. It's too strong to attempt to sleep again.

Out of curiosity, she moves the light around the room. Nothing unusual jumps out at her. There's no dark shadow lurking out in the hall either. She and June are alone in this room in this old manor.

By now the smell is bearable and she hardly notices it anymore. That's the good news for tonight.

And yet it doesn't outweigh the bad news she's just discovered.

Her eyes squint in the darkness of the room. She maneuvers the blankets off her legs to crawl a little way up her bed to lean over the edge slightly.

July fails to see whatever it is that her flashlight caught over on June's side.

After taking a deep breath, she climbs off the bed fully.

She's really careful about how she steps over the wood floor, fear leaking into her body.

You see, one day a while ago when June was out late due to cheer practice, July stepped all over this room to figure out which old boards made the most noise. Now more than ever she is so grateful for her thinking ahead. There's little possibility that she'll wake up June and cause her sister to go madder than normal.

Once safely across the room she aims the light right onto what seems to be a cluster of various weeds growing through the cracks in the floorboards. Despite the semi-unusual environment for them they seem to be quite healthy.

They've got rich green stems and soft leaves. Her hands itch to touch a few of them. Before she gives into this strange urge, she raises the light to discover the weeds also growing out of cracks on the wall.

"What the fuck?" Her words are a whisper into this cold night.

July gets off her crouched knees in awe. These weeds create an almost perfect circle around June's bed. How did either of them not notice before going to bed?

None of this should be possible now that she's thinking about it. Sure, some plants grow overnight. But certainly no weeds through the second floor of the manor.

She shakes her head slowly. This must be apart from all the noises and smell. There is no other explanation. All that's left to figure out is why. The how really isn't that important to her.

There is of course the idea that she is in fact sleeping and only imagining June's discomfort. She had been reading about local plant life. This is perhaps a manifestation of what she's learned. She's going to go with that weak theory until something worse comes along to convince her otherwise.

July places the flashlight on her bed, making sure its beam doesn't get into June's face. She stopped fussing in her sleep. Her soft snores fill the room.

She doesn't waste time ripping the weeds from the floor and walls. At first, they refused to leave their new home after mustering all her force and accidently bumping her already fucked up knee.

It takes her the rest of the night to do this and make sure none of the evidence lingers. No one else has to know about this.

July doesn't get back in bed till the sun starts rising with dirty fingers.

# 9. The Warning

July sits on the porch with her satchel next to her. Her hand clutches the strap for dear life. She doesn't want to get up. She doesn't want to leave this house for longer than she needs to.

It might do something dangerous without them being there.

The winter winds blow across the lawn that's surrounded by many tall dead trees. Their red and yellow and orange leaves fell way before they arrived in Swamp Hill.

It glides through her unbound hair like lanky fingers as well as caress her neck and flushed face.

A coldness lingers about. Nothing unusual about it. However, it does its best to bite into her exposed flesh. Leaving her with bright pink cheeks and chapped lips.

At least her glasses protect her eyes from drying out like a drought.

"C'mon, July. We ain't got all day to wait on your ass." June's shout from the running truck echoes into the air.

She registers the words but still makes no move to get off the porch steps no matter how they're screamed at her.

There's something about this house, this town that feels off.

July isn't ready to explore more of it and find something she wasn't initially looking for. Now that would suck ass.

Their mother huffs in the driver's seat.

"Look, if there's a bookstore, I'll let you buy two books. How does that sound?" Abigail unknowingly stoops low with this bribe.

July furrows her brows. They lower over her narrowing eyes. Anger courses through her.

Of course, it sounds absolutely tempting. And yet she rather not be alone in this troubling manor either. Damn. There are no good options, are there?

With a sharp inhale, she carefully stands. She makes sure not to lock her knees. That happened once and she face planted within moments which marked her second emergency room visit for a broken nose.

The breeze almost seems to guide her towards the truck where the heater's on and running. The inside must be toasty. It's a clear escape from this place.

She's having trouble thinking that this is the best idea. And yet neither of them have seen what she's been a witness to. July isn't going to tell them either. It would confuse them and make her out to be a nutjob.

"I'm coming." She pulls her jacket tighter over her chest and limps to the truck.

July hasn't taken the time to look out of the bus window on the way to and home from school. There hasn't been any urge to gaze upon the town. Maybe that was a mistake. Perhaps she can fix it now.

The main part of town is filled with locally owned shops and restaurants.

Abigail parks the truck in the parking lot, big enough to host the entire town. It leads to the main street and has easy access to the sidewalks.

"I'm in need of new jeans and a few blouses." June huffs.

She curled her hair again. The bouncy strands settle on her shoulders that are covered in a light blue coat that pairs nicely with her eyes.

Abigail nods her head instantly. "Sure, we can do that. What about you, July?"

She snaps out of her little trance and offers a crooked smile.

"No thanks. I'm going to find a bookstore." She keeps her voice small. Being careful not to steal any of June's much-needed spotlight.

Her sister scoffs loudly, pulling their mother's attention away back on her. Such an original move. July rolls her eyes.

"Okay, we'll be around these little thrift places and such. Come find us when you found something you want to get, okay?" Abigail attempts to place her hand atop July's shoulders.

The young girl steps back in a rush, barely missing the edge of the curb. Abigail hurries to snatch the front of her jacket.

"Fucking clutz." June mumbles with a voice loud enough for their mother to hear.

Abigail twirls around quickly. She's got that rare fuming expression on her face.

"Watch your mouth and be nicer to your sister. I don't need y'all fighting today. We are here to have a nice time and enjoy each other's company." She does her best to make the situation better.

All it does is cause July to flush with embarrassment and self-pity. She doesn't need or want Abigail to fight her battles. She never has and won't ever.

The rage swarming in her chest decides to lash out.

"Fuck you, June." She spits at her sister before storming off in the opposite direction.

She ignores Abigail's painful shouts and June's cursing. She does everything to block them both out of her head.

Of course, they can't go anywhere without fighting. That's how it's always been. However, usually the fights end with them with busted lips and scratches all over their red faces.

Her hair whips around her chilled face as she crosses the street in search of perhaps one of the few places on Earth that she feels welcome in.

Even that sounds so fucking lonely.

After searching for maybe an hour she stumbles upon a little shop at the very end of the main street.

From what she can see the inside lights are purposely dimmed to show off the many candle lights. Their flickering wicks illuminate many stacks and shelves of books lining the dark brick walls and velvety brown carpet.

A smile grows on her face. Her heart no longer thumps like a mad rabbit. She can finally have some peace.

She needed to find this. Maybe it was waiting for her to find it.

As she reaches for the door handle another hand collides with hers. It's an accident but one that greatly startles her.

"Oh, I'm so sorry." July rushes to say, bowing her head automatically to avoid eye contact.

"No apology needed." The other person chuckles softly.

Her eyes grow wide, lashing upward to be touched by a small smile that graces her lips. She pushes her glasses up with jittery fingers. She allows excitement to coat her bones and warm her chest.

Ms. Tibbs stands there next to July with a soft grin and an arm full of books.

"Let me get the door for you." July hurries to grip the handle to pull it open. Carrying those must cause the woman's arm to ache.

The librarian mutters a quick thank you before entering the bookstore.

July watches her and the other older woman behind the counter greet each other. It's good that they know one another. It may mean more bookish friends for July to meet. That's not really a bad thing.

Her mother would rejoice at the idea. There she goes again. Thinking of what others think of her or what she does. She really needs to stop that. June does enough of it for her.

She follows Ms. Tibbs and helps her put the books back on their various shelves. It isn't hard to figure out the sorting system. Most of the bookcases are labeled with genre and certain letters from the alphabet. A plain categorization that anyone could understand. That is if they aren't stupid.

Her thoughts on this waver to June.

Then they pick a couch in the far back with pretty little lamps shaped like flowers shining down upon them.

July places down her bag to her feet before saying, "I've been dying to get out of that house. You know, Birkstone Manor. Something about that place gives me the creeps."

It may have been a few days since she started hanging in the library with the woman, but she still gets excited to talk with her only friend in this truly boring town.

"Weird noises keep going bump in the night. And there's been this awful smell that I can't seem to find a source for. I swear, the more I'm in that house the worse everything gets. I have no idea how my sister or mom hasn't noticed it too." July keeps talking, moving her hands with each word she speaks.

A flood of ease courses through her bones. She's been wishing to talk to someone about this. Good thing it's to Ms. Tibbs. Now that woman isn't afraid of trouble.

She may know how to help her figure this mysterious phenomenon out.

And yet she suddenly wishes she kept her mouth shut. July gulps and sinks into the green suede cushion.

Ms. Tibbs adjusts her glasses as well. Her eyes narrowing from either agitation or disappointment. Looks that July has trouble distinguishing from one another.

Damnit.

Once a screwup, always a screwup. Another famed June Birkstone line.

"If I said something that offended you, I didn't mean anything by it. I swear." Beads of sweat beg to trickle down the sides of her face.

Is the heater on in this place? It's awfully warm here.

"You need to stay away from the purple door. People in this town may be already watching you and your family. It would be best for you all to pack your things and leave." Ms. Tibbs leans forward from the opposite couch to tell her this.

Her brows rise almost to her hair line. She runs a trembling hand through her hair, moving it over her left shoulder and out of her eyes.

July gives a snort of sorts. A sound someone makes when they're in a state of shock and disbelief.

"I...uhh...didn't mention a door." Her words are whispers.

The librarian says nothing. She ignores July completely. She reaches for a book that was left on the cushion next to her and curiously flips pages in it.

July pays her no mind when jumping up and running out of the store and back on the sidewalk.

Despite her limp, she runs as if she's being chased. That's what this feeling in her chest is like. That someone or something is gaining on her and she has just moments to get away.

She knew that something wasn't right. Now she knows for certain that the door in the corn is involved.

But how? Why? So many possible answers that she doesn't want to find.

# 10. Missing Sis

She was the first to make it back to the truck and the first to get out of it when they parked in front of Birkstone Manor.

They had homemade chili and yeast rolls for supper. It lacked flavor due to Abigail doing all the cooking. But it filled the empty hole in her belly anyway.

She needed something for her twisting stomach to cling onto other than her sanity.

Going to sleep wasn't too hard this time either. The moment her head hit the pillow she was out like a light. No dreams or strange sounds came to haunt her in the cold night. Nor do any strange smells slip into her nose when she's least expecting them to.

At least not right away, that is.

July woke with a troubling start.

She heard that damn creaking sound again in her sleep. Only this time it came from the foot of her bed. Sleep wasn't doing much good after that.

As she rises beneath her many blankets and casually looks over to June's side her breath halts entirely. The heart in her frail chest stalls, skipping beats like a river rapid. She anxiously rubs the scar between her breasts, wishing that agitating sting would go away.

June's bed is completely empty. Her comforter and sheets were thrown to the floor. For some reason, her silky pink night gown is on top of the mess as well along with faintly used underwear.

Where is she? How long has she been gone?

She quickly gets out of her own bed, leaving the warm sheets and comfy blankets.

July fetches her jacket, pulling it over her pajama shirt. She hurries to slip on a pair of boots meant for rain. Harsh drops pelt the outside of the house. It's a hammering noise that most likely won't be letting up any time soon.

God, she hopes June isn't out with friends in this harsh weather. Her worry might cost her a slap to the face but at least June would be right in front of her to cause any pain.

The town looks like it's particularly vulnerable to flooding.

Before leaving the safety of their room July clutches her flashlight and stuffs one of her spare inhalers into her jacket pocket. It might come in handy if she encounters anything remotely dangerous that causes her to panic and lose her breath.

She makes sure to step light when entering the dark hallway.

Lightning from the outside shines through the window, casting the walls in an array of colors from the stained glass.

Most of the rooms have been closed to conserve heat. Which means she's going to have to open the doors herself very carefully. A damn racoon can run out with its young following behind for all she knows. The woods and swamps are far closer than she likes them to be.

July takes a steady breath, allowing her lungs to inflate, filling the organs to their brim before letting it back out.

As she raises her hand to grasp the first door's handle, a rattling begins. It's coming from within her. It might be her fear or sudden unease. Two emotions that feel too distinct for this moment.

This is the large broom closet that's meant to keep the floor stocked with things like toilet paper and bath towels.

She releases a startling breath. Nothing sinister lurking in here. Time to move onto the next room.

Somehow, with each room being empty it gets easier to check the entire house. Well, she avoids the attic and basement. She doubts June would venture off to those even in her worst state of mind. Her sister would find them icky and scream if she ran into a cobweb. More than anything stuffy places that mess with her curled hair would send her into a coma for sure.

July huffs loudly. The sound bounces off the walls in the living room. She wishes she knew how to light the fireplace. It's so cold here that her breath fogs before her face.

June isn't in the house. She remembers seeing her purse sitting on her vanity so she can't be out with her friends either. Then where the hell is she?

Her eyes grow wide at a new thought that sprouts in her mind.

No. There's no way that she might…

She gulps nervously. Sweat brought on by fear gathers at the back of her neck and in her palms. Without thinking she wipes them onto her plaid pajama pants.

Her steps are terribly slow as she makes way to the back door. The muscles in her jaw tick from her clenching it shut too hard. It creates a pain that grounds her frightened mind.

The storm lightning illuminates the cornfield, making it easy to scan the stalks.

Birkstone Manor sits high enough to get a look at the entire field and everything in it. Including the purple door where June is standing in front of completely naked!

"June!" She shouts at the same time as a clash of thunder booms in the dark grey clouds that roll in the distance.

July rushes down the slippery stone steps, managing to catch herself before slipping on the last one and faceplanting in the mud.

She should have put on her glasses for this. But there was no time. There's no chance to turn back now and let her sister suffer in the freezing rain.

No matter how cruel June is, she's still July's sister. Her twin.

The girl weaves through the stalks. It proves difficult to remember the path they took that led them to the door in the first place. Every turn and all the twists in the corn look the exact same.

When she thinks she finds a way to the center she's lead right in the opposite direction. Damnit, it's hopeless!

It offers her a random thought she never considered before. Perhaps someone planted the corn stalks like this on purpose. To keep people from reaching the purple door or to keep something in. Oh, fuck.

The thought quickly becomes a realization as she hurries in circles, eventually forcing her way through the many rows. Not once taking account of the many scratches and bruises now being left on her skin. Her pajamas and jacket must be shredded from this.

None of it will matter if she can't get to June.

At last, she pushes through the last bit of corn that separates them. By now the rain has stopped. All that's left in its wake is mud and loose gravel.

It leaves an uneven path to her sister.

She's still standing in front of it. Her body shivers like a damn chihuahua crapped out on acid.

"June?" Her words are soft, not meant to startle her sister and cause her to freak out.

*"Blood is gift. Shadow is power. Blood is gift. Shadow is power. Blood. Blood. Blooodd…."* Her words make no sense and are beginning to slur.

July momentarily hides away her sanity as she takes off her ruined jacket to drape it over June's shaking shoulders.

The movement wakes June in an instant. She stops muttering. Her wide red eyes darting around the door and field only to land on July. Her lips shift into a snarl.

Hell, she'll take that over a fucking zombie sister any day.

She nods her head slowly. "June, I found you like this. Are you alright? Does anything hurt or feel funny?"

After various doctor visits over the years and complicated surgeries she's picked up on a few phrases all the doctors and surgeons liked to use. They didn't have to dumb it down for her but maybe they'll come in handy for this.

"You found me naked in the cornfield?" She laughs at herself in a raspy tone.

July gives her a puzzled look. She's not feeling well at all by the looks of it.

June has never had eye bags in her entire life. And yet they're large and dark purple that seem to drain life out of her face. July isn't going to say anything to her about it. She'll go nuts and certainly hit her on the arm a few times before crashing out.

She shakes her head to get a grip on herself and this strange situation.

"Look, I woke up and found your bed empty. You're lucky I didn't leave your ass out here to freeze to death. The rain could have swept you away." She says and shoots the door a glare.

Her sister gives her a hmm and nothing more. She tugs the jacket around her exposed shoulders tighter to block out the frigid air. Not even an eyeroll. This is so bizarre.

"I was sleepwalking and must have got stuck out here. And no, I wouldn't have been swept away by the rain because it wasn't raining." She says in a matter-of-fact way.

Now it's July's turn to scoff at her words. "Of course it was raining. It was thundering and lightening all night."

Her sister turns to her, giving her the worst frown of her life, and starts walking away as if nothing ever happened.

July shakes her head. It was raining. She seen and smelled the rain. So fresh that even the local cows could clear their sinuses.

And yet as she looks at the ground to find it dry, tears leak from her eyes. June has gotten back into the house by now, so she won't be waiting for July to stop her crying.

This doesn't make any sense. It was raining. Storming, even. Wasn't it?

No, she can't be losing her mind now. Not like this.

She crouches down to touch the dry dirt with her hands. She cups some and lets it fall between her fingers.

This isn't right at all. Then how can this explain her wet clothes-

Her eyes expand in fear. July's pajamas aren't damp at all. There's no drop of anything on them. She's completely fine. It's not possible.

A striking breath fans across the back of her neck. She whips around to find herself alone.

Her heart beats within her ribcage fast. It feels like it might burst through her chest as a fist. Damn, she might puke from all this adrenaline pumping in her body.

The corn is still standing tall and harbors no one else besides her. Nothing to be afraid of. And yet she knows there's something out there. Someone or something watching her. They have been since they moved in.

Oh, she's totally going insane.

Clouds shift in the sky, letting the moonlight cascade and make the damn door glow.

July rises off her knees. She dusts her hands slowly while not taking her eyes off it.

She refuses to let her mind wonder why this door is here and why the corn was created to be a maze to keep people away from it.

Despite the harsh throb in her knee, she limps to the house down the clear path leading to the porch.

# Part II

# 11. Friday Night Frights

The first week attending this new school shouldn't have gone so terribly as it did. July finding her sister in the middle of the cornfield towards the end of it wasn't expected either.

She couldn't tell Abigail about it this morning. The words didn't sit right on her tongue. It's not her strange story to tell.

As they sit at the kitchen table with bowls of sugary grits in front of them, she keeps her damn mouth shut. Every time she glances at June, she's already giving July a heated glare.

*Yeah. Keep your mouth shut, July. I'll skin you alive if you so much as blink funny.*

That's what her creepy vacant eyes seemed to say. The blue tint to them doesn't sparkle like it usually does. Even her cheeks seem oddly boney. June may normally be thin but today something's different about her.

July can't put her finger quite on it yet.

And so that's what July does. She keeps shoving spoonfuls of the grounded corn into her mouth, ignoring the texture that doesn't agree with her stomach.

Abigail didn't feel like cooking gooey scrambled eggs, hickory smoked bacon, and the softest of biscuits with creamy white peppered gravy like she sometimes does.

But this is much better than going hungry or worse, having to find something in the cafeteria when they get to school later.

Speaking of school, today is not filled with the usual sour words from June and her friends or their moves to trip her with every given opportunity. They avoid her. Make sure not to look in her direction even during passing periods.

It's easy to guess the reason for it. Tonight is the last football game of the season. The team lost their last playoff game, but the school wants to put on another game for the senior class. But this one they aren't playing against another team. The principle is splitting the players to play against themselves.

A truly bizarre thing.

One last hurrah or some shit like that.

July thought nothing about it until the lack of mean words shot her way.

Her sister must have said she's a bad luck charm if they even look at her.

Now that has a pleasant ring to it. She's poor June's bad luck charm. If only she knew that she's the same for July. They are perfectly crafted to ruin each other. They're twins. They will always be each other's downfall. One of the faulty perks of being born from the same mother at the same time during a once-in-a-lifetime solar eclipse.

Ms. Tibbs for some reason avoids her too.

When she got to the library during her lunch hour the librarian was nowhere to be found. She spent that lonely period eating a cold turkey sandwich her mother packed and began reading a new book about the effects of climate change in Texas.

On the way home on the bus July realized her sister never got on with her.

Normally she wouldn't care what June does but after what happened last night, she's grown worried. They haven't really talked about it either. But what is there to say? She found June sleepwalking without any clothes on. And rain that she was almost certain that fell never actually dropped from the sky at all? Yeah, sounds like the best conversation to have.

"Hey, mom!" She shouts into the house as soon as she gets through the front door.

Any other day she'd call her Abigail, but she needs her most undivided attention.

The woman in question pops into the living room from the kitchen. Her hands, face and the front of her red and green flannel are covered in white power. Flour by the looks of it.

July gives her a confused grimace.

Abigail's brows furrows before she looks at herself. Her high pitch laughter then bounces off the walls, threatening to shake all the taxidermy that covers most of the wallpaper in the living room.

She shakes her head. "What did you need, July? Did something happen at school again? Damnit, I told June to cut you some slack."

July quickly dismisses her concerns. A new heat settles in her chest, clinging to her ribs like a warm hug filled with dread.

"It's just that June wasn't on the bus. I was thinking maybe you had picked her up from school early. I'm guessing that's not the case either." She releases a staggering breath.

Abigail nods as she takes in her daughter's words.

She teers on the balls of her feet. The ticking of a clock somewhere in the house suddenly takes over the awkward atmosphere.

Usually, both July and Abigail avoid each other. They never formed a connection. At least not one like June and their mother has. But she's not envious of it. That's just the way it is.

And yet now it's revealing the strange nature of their unconventional mother–daughter relationship.

She blames herself for it most of the time. Not once has she ever asked for help unless she absolutely needed it. Of course, Abigail, being who she is, always noticed when July felt unwell or had broken another bone. Only then did she truly jump into Mother Mode and whisk her away to the emergency room.

So, in a way, her feelings were never hurt by what June and their mother shared. She was a parent to her when it was called for. No hard feeling on that.

"She probably stayed after school to get ready at Trudy Stone's house. You know her mother likes to host weekend sleepovers for the cheer team after every home game. Well, that's what your principal told me when I first went up there to speak with the nurse about your emergency allergy meds and backup inhaler. But usually, she would have called to tell me they made it over there by now. Huh. That's strange, isn't it?" Abigail twiddles her thumbs, causing flour to drift onto the dark wood floor.

July bites her bottom lip in frustration. This conversation has now turned pointless.

It's going to be dark in a few hours. The town is going to go wild from this football game. And if June hasn't called the landline by then something must be wrong. She just senses it.

She offers her mother a strained smile before saying she'll go to the game later and check on June.

Abigail sounds utterly surprised and yet gleeful about this idea of hers. Hell, as July limps up the stairs she shouts how proud of her she is for making sure June's okay.

Not long after that her mother starts playing the radio with 90s hits spilling into the manor.

It's no surprise that June didn't call the landline. In fact, that's what July was counting on. An excuse to get out of this fucking creepy mansion for one night and keep June from ruining other people's lives for once.

Now that may be a big hope to have. However, it's all that's fueling July in the race to the game.

Abigail gave her a quick rundown of how to drive the damn truck. It's not hard to shift a gear and steer the wheel in whatever direction she needs to go in. A piece of pecan pie, really.

How hard can it really be?

But the second July gets in the driver seat dressed in loose fitted jeans, a terribly knitted dark green sweater and her jacket and she already feels defeated. This is a big fucking mistake.

Why must it take her a solid five minutes just to figure out the heater?

She quits messing with the center console and just says fuck it. She's got more important things to worry about than freezing to death on the way back to school.

July drives through town very slowly. Angry shouts from those zooming past her are all that keeps her company. Every thought she's got is negative and of the worst possibilities there are. None of them attempt to fizzle into something lighter and warmer. Her insides are chilled not only from the night but of what June may be doing right now.

She easily welcomes the impatient honks directed towards her. They act as echo location in way or some shit like that, reminding her that she is in the truck and on the way to find her sister. All the streetlights and headlights glare on her glasses, blinding her almost. The honks either tell her she's too close to someone's back bumper or not going fast enough.

Damnit. She can't win at all in this situation. She never wanted to be in this mess.

And yet none of it matters anymore when she finally pulls into the overfilled parking lot of the high school stadium. Shit. Maybe this isn't a good idea after all.

There's nothing she can do about it now.

She's forced to park on the very edge of the lot. Right in the dry grass that desperately begs for rain. She still isn't sure of whether it was raining when finding June in the cornfield. Her mind is slowly being scrambled.

July stalks through the many rows of large trucks and old timey cars to get to the front gates that lead into the home side stands.

The man dressed in their school colors asks for her student ID. She quickly fishes it out of her jacket pocket, making sure to remember that the same pocket contains her backup allergy pills and inhaler.

Once he confirms her identity, July rushes past him and into the game. She hears him shouting at her telling her to stop running. Well, she wouldn't call her hobbled jog a run, but she ignores his warning anyway.

Loud roars from the crowd and tremendously bad school band music flood her ears. The game has only just started and already there are people acting like lunatics.

She never understood the sport and doesn't want too ever. It's an utter waste of time. There are more important things to invest in such as studying and preparing for college entrance exams.

July rushes to the fence bordering the field and track. She spots the cheerleaders in an instant as they continue kicking their legs and shaking their poms. None of their chants make a lick of sense and yet the crowd eats it up and go feral as they decide to toss school shirts and mini footballs into the stands.

As she leans close, she sees that June isn't among them like she was hoping.

"Shit." She hisses in desperation.

The girl tugs at the end of her braid and moves in another direction. Maybe June is taking a break and getting something to eat at the concession stand. She can smell the nacho cheese and sour pickles from here. It makes her stomach gurgle.

She observes the lines closely. There's been a few blondes who've stepped up to order sour candy straws and the occasional hotdog, but none are the calculating and cruel June. They lack her overly vibrant voice and bouncing personality. And her sister wouldn't be caught dead letting these football players follow her around if she wasn't interested in them.

June does have some self-respect from what she's seen.

"Fuck." July groans, readying to move on.

She then searches every stall in both the men and women's bathrooms. No sign of her there either. A few people weren't happy as she ducked under the door to see inside their stall. More than a few couples were getting down and dirty.

She muttered a quick apology before moving on.

All that's left to check is the stands. Both in and under them. She'll force herself to search the crowd first to get it over with.

Of course, she receives angry shouts from them to get out of the way or find an old folk's home to stay in. Even the grownups of this town know about her somewhat hindered stature.

Well, fuck them ten ways to Sunday.

July shivers from the dropping temperature as she limps towards the underneath of all the metal stands that vibrate from excited stomping. It sounds like someone on the team made a touchdown from the sudden boom that makes her bones tremble.

She searches behind various trashcans and the closed merchandise booth before almost giving up.

But then her ears pick up on something that may be a lead. There's a strange smacking sound coming from the abandoned supplies shed at the edge of the field.

From what she's heard during her time in class the head coaches have stopped using it for whatever reason that she can't recall at the moment.

July carefully steps towards it. Her chest is heaving with strangled breaths. This jacket is suddenly too constricting. But if she takes it off then she'll catch a serious cold and end up in the hospital again.

She refuses to feel weak like that once more.

There is no light shining from the small window made into the old wood door that's seen better days. It's cracked and missing a few pieces too.

July inhales the chilled air and lets her breath shift into a fog.

The noise morphs into a pained groan. Her heart takes a lurch. It sounded oldy high pitched. Oh, shit!

"June!" She shouts in a rush, feeling panicked that her sister may be hurt inside.

She's quick on her feet to rip the door open and flip the light switch she manages to find on the wall to her right.

It's her sister alright, dressed in a ruffled cheer uniform and her hair in a loose braid. She's fiercely making out with a band kid by the looks of his t-shirt.

Maybe his name is Chuck? She can't quite define his face with June's head in the way.

But from what she can see in her stunned state is June wiggling her hand around in the boy's pants. Oh, that's totally gross. July swallows down a gag that tries to rise in her throat.

June seems to be humping his leg as well. This is so fucked. Why does this have to happen?

"Get the fuck off him!" July hisses. Clearly her sister needs to go home and sleep whatever the fuck this is off.

The sudden noise startles them both. June staggers backward in a daze. The boy who is most certainly Chuck, whimpers. He was, is, in pain.

July brings a hand to her gaping mouth. Her eyes going wide at the disheveled bloody sight of him.

The front of his band shirt is covered in blood that continues to flood from his bottom lip. June must have spilt it with her own teeth. Her stomach lurches. She gulps down the bile that rose in her throat.

He doesn't get the chance to run off, not yet. July quickly grabs his shirt. The blood that's still warm generously smearing on her hands.

She looks into his watery blue eyes and snarls, "Keep your mouth shut. Alright? She's on some kind of drug that's laced with something shitty."

Chuck believes in an instant. Thank fuck. His head nods frantically, logging the dangerous drug excuse in his mind. She knows he'll talk and say what she said. Kids like him are so gullible. Fear is a great conduit for influence compulsion, allowing weakened minds to absorb anything that's being told to them whether it's true or false. She hopes it will work like she wants it to.

She tosses him back, telling him to get the hell out of here.

June stumbles a little. She's not really in the moment. Her mind is somewhere else.

"We gotta go home now, June." She hurries to take off her jacket and throws it over her sister's trembling shoulders.

There's a sense of deja vu that tugs at her chest. She ignores it completely. Refusing to think of last night.

"Please, take my hand." July swallows thickly. Her eyes now sting with unshed tears.

June's a mess. A sight she rarely sees. But this time it's different. Something serious is the matter with her. And she doesn't think it can be explained by any doctor.

With a soft tired expression, June takes her hand and lets July lead her out of the shed, underneath the stadium stands, and back to the truck.

At this hour there are no other cars on the roads. Making it easy and safer to drive through. July takes occasional glances at her sister who fell asleep as soon as her head touched the seat.

Abigail is already in bed when they arrive at Birkstone Manor. None of the lights are on inside and their mother's white noise machine echoes a lovely classical tune throughout the halls.

She takes time to get June up the steps, afraid of stepping on the wrong piece of wood that may creak and wake their mother. No need for her to come out to investigate why they're home early from the game.

July can figure this out on her own.

After cleaning the blood off June's face and hands, getting her into a simple pink night gown with frilly lace sleeves, she tucks her into bed.

Even gives her a soft kiss upon her cheek before turning off the room light.

She knows that when June wakes, she'll be back to her normal hateful self.

# 12. The White Deer

For the past several nights after the football game incident June hasn't acted odd at all. In fact, she wished for July to have a good night before turning off their room light. It was one of the most bizarre interactions she's ever had with her.

July hasn't found the nerve to ask June if she wants to talk about it either. She assumes that her sister is doing her best to forget it. She doesn't blame her for that.

She too would want to take that confusing and scary memory to the far corner of her mind.

Seeing all that blood and lost expression in her eyes has July watching her more closely than ever before.

But each night July wakes up and finds June's bed empty once again. It was easy to determine where she was quickly.

July found her sister naked, again standing before the door with a lost haze over her eyes and muttering that nonsense.

There had been no mysterious storms to go bump in the night that later had all traces of it disappear.

And tonight is really no different except that July is prepared for it.

The small silver alarm clock on her night table chimes when the hands strike three. The witching hour or some shit like that. It barely does anything to wake her, she is up before it screams in the chilled night anyways.

This time she puts on an old pair of cowgirl boots before trudging out into the field. She brings a blanket with her the size of the living room floor almost. It's heavy and thick with a fleece material that instantly traps June's body heat the second she drapes it over her.

June wakes softly. The cloud over her eyes dissipates in a flash. But it's not enough for July to think her sister's okay. This shouldn't be happening at all.

In just those two short weeks she's dropped weight. The pounds have just slithered off her bones and muscles. She can see June's ribs poke through all her cute pink shirts and frilly skirts. Even those hang off her malnourished body. Sometimes she can hear her sister puking in the bathroom.

It's unsettling.

The worst downfall imaginable of June Birkstone.

Her limbs can be mistaken for a spider's. That's how tragic she looks. Even their mother has spoken up about it. Wondering if June is going far enough to skip lunch and breakfast when they're at school.

Of course, her sister being the queen bitch of all bitches, she lashes out and spits in Abigail's face like it's nothing. Not the most fascinating time spent in Birkstone Manor.

"July?" June asks as they start to turn away from the purple door.

She stalls them for a moment. Gazing upon her frail sister who looks worse than her. And July is known for looking sickly, unfortunately.

July slowly nods her head. Encouraging her sister to say something else. Anything is better than this wicked silence. It's torture.

"I had the strangest dream. Something was calling to me in the darkness. I did my best not to let it get me. But it did, July. Claws sinking into my back, pulling me into the dark with it. I was so scared. I'm still scared." She takes note of the way June glances back to the purple door, somehow afraid of it.

It only further fuels her suspicions.

July doesn't follow her gaze. She will be strong for both of them and get them out of whatever the fuck this is.

She begins to guide her towards the porch steps.

Deep grey clouds blanket the sky, trapping the half-moon and its fair blue light behind it. And yet she can still perfectly see the white deer that steps out from behind the door that has been somehow causing these problems.

She gulps. Swallowing her sudden fear and anger that she directs toward it. Maybe it can feel her pain. July hopes it can experience some sort of guilt.

Why would such a precious looking creature with horns that spiral skyward like towers be near this place at all? How come she hasn't seen it before? It makes no sense.

July keeps her mouth shut and continues helping June to the stairs and into the house.

However, she stays on the porch by herself to gaze at this deer. Its eyes are wide and are the shade of molten emerald. They're so big that she can see the tears welling in them, dripping along its velvet-like white coat.

Her own eyes squint in a flash of anger. It swells in her chest, invading her body's blood vessels and such. A feeling that's certainly thrilling.

She watches it bow its majestic head slightly to the right toward the door. The movement filled with something she cannot determine sparks her own steps off the porch and back into the cornfield to face it.

"What does it mean? What is the door doing to her? Tell me!" She whispers shouts at it, spit flying from her lips at the force of her words.

A small whimper comes from it. He or she gives her nothing else to go on. It scampers away like a coward and leaves her to wallow in her many theories and questions. She hopes it also possesses the ability to experience guilt. Why stand there and look upon her with such emotion and flee when it clearly knows something?

What a pathetic animal.

July curses and flips it the bird.

She fumes when storming into the house. She makes sure to lock every door and window that leads to her and June's room. Nothing is going to get in on her watch.

# 13. Butterflies?

"I can't believe I let your dumbass convince me to take a stroll." June's words are lethal as if they're laced with poison and tipped with sharp arrowheads.

July rolls her eyes at the insult. The words, however, slip off her shoulders like the air itself. She stopped taking everything June says personally after the first time she found her in the field.

The long gravel driveway that leads to and from Birkstone Manor is rustled by the late winter winds. It's been causing all kinds of dust and pollen to swirl around them brought from distant fields. Her eyes are unwillingly watery from it all getting in them.

She's sneezed seven times since leaving the manor. Yes, she counted.

June is wrapped in a thick pink corduroy jacket with a pale blue sweater underneath it. Her black jeans flare above her shoes like she's a famous super star.

She on the other hand is in her jacket with loose dark jeans that fail to hug her boney legs. Abigail wouldn't let her out of the house without wearing a beanie. July chose to wear the one with little vines embroidered on it.

It's decent to look at. Not a real eye catcher. Just how she prefers.

"Check the mail while we're out here. Might as well make yourself useful." June checks her fingernails after gesturing at the end of the driveway.

July gives a huff instead of trying to go against the order. She'll comply, for now.

She fishes out the mail and finds things from three days ago. Abigail must have been forgetting to check it after getting home from her new job. Her mother found this small boutique in town that sells the most Southern clothes you've ever seen.

All kinds of turquoise and bellbottom jeans. It's disgusting.

When she turns around with the various colored envelopes in hand, she can only just see June walking into the manor without her.

"Bitch." She mumbles only to herself.

July tried to say it once in front of her and June smacked her so hard in the face she momentarily blacked out. That was the worst black eye she'd ever given her.

She turns to make sure she got everything out. After nodding to herself that she did in fact get all the mail, she turns again only this time gasping in fright.

At least a thousand monarch butterflies line the singular lamppost. Others sit on the many tree branches and cover the cornfield fence that peak through the pines and oaks.

Were they there before? Have they been watching her and June this entire time? That doesn't seem plausible. She would have seen them way earlier.

She moves her foot in front of the other very slowly, keeping her breath to a steady rhythm, afraid to spook these creatures. They seem to be waiting for something. But what could it be?

From what she's read about Texas wildlife, they shouldn't even be in the state so far into winter. Thousands of them have already migrated south.

However, the second her foot accidentally snaps a lone twig they freak.

July rushes forth with all these beautiful butterflies hot on her tail.

They gather her in a brutal swarm, their little legs tickling her face and hands. Some manage to thinly slice any area of exposed skin. Her face and hands are on fire.

With a screech, she drops the mail and runs fast, or as fast as her limp will allow her to go.

She's at least twenty feet from the porch steps. Her heart stutters at the sight of June smirking down at her, standing on the porch just watching it all happen.

July stops abruptly at this look. Her body clams up. Fear that consumes her belly, acting like a fire inside her, claws everything else. And yet it's caused by her sister who seems to enjoy watching her be tormented by these little fucking bugs.

Within a second, June's smirk melts into a shout. "Mom, the butterflies are after July!"

That is the most humiliating thing of all. People are going to help her when she doesn't need or want it. It's the worst and June knows it better than anyone. What the fuck is wrong with this bitch?

She staggers forward, her left foot catching on an exposed tree root that she's just now noticing. How tragic.

The front door opens again just as these fucking bugs scatter to the winds, leaving her alone finally and covered in itty bitty scratches.

Abigail hurries out. Her wide blue eyes searching within this scene that's truly pathetic.

"T-The butterflies came out of nowhere. They attacked m-me. June, you just left me." She says breathlessly.

Her sister shrugs. "I didn't see anything. You must have fell and hit your head."

July's brows pull back in surprise. She knows her sister is cruel already but acting like she's the nutjob is wild.

Abigail shakes her head, somehow telling herself that July would of course do something like this.

"I'm not a damn cripple! Abigail? Mom!" She tries to shrug the older woman off.

It does no good. She calls upon June to help July up the steps. Their hold on her almost too tight.

"It's the fucking truth!" She shouts as they shove her inside the house.

Her chest heaves. Tears leak down her face. Why won't her mother believe her? She's not a liar for fuck's sake.

July has always been the best student and the almost good daughter who stuffers medically. Never has she done something so crazy as to lie for the fun of it. That's all June. She is the daughter, the student, and the sister that does whatever to get her way.

And what is her way, exactly? Perhaps to ruin what little reputation July has? If so, then she's doing a bang-up job.

Abigail makes her get out of her chilled clothes and into warm pajamas she threw into the dryer for a few minutes. Yes, her hands and face may sting from the small paper cuts she received from the butterflies and their spiney legs, but not because she tripped.

Hell, she did trip. But she knows for a fact she didn't hit her head. Not even a little bit. Landing in gravel would do more bruising than cutting. It's obvious.

"Look, let's forget this happened and focus on something more positive, yeah? The dance is a few weeks away and y'all need to start looking for dresses. We'll go into town tomorrow and get to work on finding some, okay? Now, get some sleep. You need it, hun." Abigail kisses her forehead gently and tucks the heavy blankets around her.

June doesn't come to bed until the hours of the night start to feel late.

When she does, she makes sure to give July a sinister grin before slipping underneath her pretty sheets.

July shuts her eyes that night wondering if she imagined June's weight loss too because her sister was truly glowing today.

# 14. Dreamless

Her sleep is empty. No dreams filled with strange horror break her from her slumber. July isn't sure if that's meant to foreshadow something much more dangerous that's supposed to find her.

The alarm next to her bed shouts into the very early morning. It awakens her blood and bones, charging her mind once more to follow through with a familiar pattern that is getting her sister inside the house and out of the cold.

But something isn't right about this night. The cold has a bite to it. Its teeth sink into her bare fingers and toes.

She doesn't find June standing in front of the purple door this time.

When July wakes to her alarm and finds June already sitting in her bed with a familiar blanket over her shoulders and puking furiously onto the floor. The noises her sister makes it enough to cause her own stomach to swirl in discomfort.

July cringes at the oddly vibrant yellow sludge that pools next to June's bed, spilling from her crusted and split lips. Damnit. Any worse and June might cough up her fucking lungs.

She pinches her nose after unwillingly receiving a waft of it. With some surprise she recognizes the foul sourness of the smell. It's like the scent that occasionally fills their room, sometimes leaking from the various weeds that grow on June's side.

It seems that every other night she cuts them from the wood floor and cracks within the wall to make sure June doesn't notice. They grew overnight. That's no exaggeration either. It's unlike anything she's read about in her books or seen in real life.

Without saying a word, July hurries to the bathroom down the unnecessarily spooky hallway and wets a few hand towels, wringing them out to where they are only just damp.

Then she cleans up the floor and June's chin and neck. Poor girl, all covered in this gross shit. July bites back a few gags, not wanting to be weird in front of June.

"My tummy hurts." June's voice is breathless. She's tired.

She must have woken up in the field all by herself before July could get to her. That realization causes her to feel truly horrible. June may be horrific on her own but not even this villain deserves whatever is happening to her.

It's not right.

July hates it with every fiber in her being.

She will get to the bottom of it. In fact, she knows the person who will certainly harbor light on this disturbing subject.

"Hey, June?" July asks across the room as she finishes tying her shoelaces.

The older twin sighs deeply. Her foul mood from last night still lingers. Good to know she still has the will to be the bitch everyone knows her to be despite throwing up the most sickening shit ever.

Of course, July hasn't said this to her. She likes all her teeth exactly where they are and not littering the floor after June hits her square in the mouth.

June flips her freshly curled hair over her shoulders. The pale strands shining like gold from the lamp lights.

When they went into town yesterday their mother stopped at the only beauty store and got June a new curl iron. No more curlers for her apparently. All July got was a new glasses case and wipes to clean the lenses.

How is that fair? Well, in a way it is completely fair. July didn't actually ask for anything. It was their mother who wanted to get this for her. She didn't gripe about it, letting the woman smile wide as she bought her youngest twin daughter something somewhat important.

"Don't start with your bullshit. I've had enough of you to last me two lifetimes." June dismisses her quickly.

July huffs and gets onto her feet. Her brows scrunch in a sudden fit.

"Will you just talk to me." She tries again.

Instead of her sister saying anything she acts in a flash.

July didn't get to see it coming. Her sister's fist decorated with dainty little rings smashes across her jaw. A searing pain shudders throughout her face and neck. The force of it shoves her down.

But June isn't done yet. Far from it.

She attempts to get up only to be stopped by a wicked kick to her chest. June's foot collides with her, sending her against her own bed.

Her spine cracks. The sound causes her to flinch. It's a loud snap. She questions if something broke that's not supposed to break. July's chest heaves as she attempts to take a proper breath.

The hits keep coming. She's got no time to duck under folded arms.

Feet kicks at her chest, stomach, and face. They don't miss their mark. When June finally pulls back to take a breath only then can she groan loudly.

Her sister gets on her knees and grips July by her ear. She hisses while being dragged up to her aching knees. Her entire body is going to be one massive bruise.

June sneers like a ferocious snake. The pupils in her pretty eyes expand wide, engulfing the whites. Then the blackness flickers into a deadly yellow shade. Same shade as the stuff she puked up last night.

Oh, shit.

July whimpers. Her fright overcoming what little bravery she had.

"Don't ever speak out of turn again. Do you understand that with your stupid, fucking pathic little mind?" June growls in her face.

She pulls back but fails to go far with her ear trapped.

She nods frantically. The flight or fight mode in her screams to flee but she can't.

How their mother didn't hear the commotion to break them apart is a mystery that she still wonders about when they get on the bus for school.

Her sister instantly sits with her friends, quickly falling into a detailed conversation about boys and hair products with Trudy. A wide smile blossoms on her peachy face. No sign of that bright yellow in her eyes. It vanished the second July complied with her.

Yeah, she's pathetic alright. No need for June to say it out loud.

That's getting old.

It can't be female monthly hormones. No. That answer is too simple. There must be something deeper that July hasn't seen yet.

This sparks more questions. She's lost count of them. She hasn't gotten around to writing them on anything. The possibility of June finding them is too great. And none of them have a plausible answer.

This sucks ass.

She listens to the students' conversations about what they had found to wear to the Senior Dance that's happening in a few weeks. Their excited chatter fails to improve her mood. Too bad the bus ride is such a long one.

Well, that's no worry for her. She isn't going. July wouldn't be caught dead in a dress of any kind. That's much more June's style.

# 15. Milky Treat

H er body aches from the provoked beating she took earlier this week. She makes sure her hair is down to cover the bruises along the sides of her neck and face. No one has spotted them, which is good.

Their mother has noticed she's been limping worse than usual. She blames it on the weather. When it gets colder in the winter months her leg acts up, the knee craps out. It isn't a complete lie.

It does happen from time to time.

Abigail went with it of course.

She walks to the library after the first lunch bell rings. However, she stops in her heated tracks to find a piece of paper taped on the closed library door.

July so desperately wanted it to be open. It's been locked all week. The paper telling her days ago that Ms. Tibbs is on vacation in Mexico to visit her family. Perhaps the worst time to be abandoned.

So badly did she want her back and explain what the fuck is wrong with the purple door and her sister.

Well, she's got two choices. Hide in an empty classroom like she's been doing or finally venture into the crowded cafeteria like all the rest of the senior and junior class.

The first option sounds nice but lately she'd been craving noise and idiocy to fill the void in her belly. The cafeteria does seem like a place that has both of those things.

What harm could it do to be there just this once?

July doesn't allow herself to dwell in the many different ways this can go wrong. She just turns around and walks away to find the source of loud voices.

This has got to be the worst idea she's ever had. Honestly, what was she thinking?

July went through the lunch line. She got a bland ham and cheese sandwich that came with a small bag of potato chips. They didn't even have any mustard packets. What assholes.

She only ate the chips and drank the stale chocolate milk that leaked from its carton as soon as she ripped it open. It dripped down the sides and on her fingers. July gave an uncomfortable squirm and left the milk unfinished.

People cleared a table the second she approached it. It was the only one in the far back with a seat open. Now she's got the whole table to herself.

It's good to assume people know who she is even though she shares the same classes with them.

June must have said to stay away from her when they first started classes. That she isn't fair game to openly be bullied without explicit permission from Queen June. No wonder they avoided her like the plague this entire time.

She will forever be the property of June Birkstone no matter that they are literally twins. A long time ago she learned to find comfort in this forever isolation.

For a good ten minutes she sat in silence and wallowed in what she likes to call Ultimate Loneliness. Don't be fooled. She enjoys this type of quiet.

It's soothing for her frazzled mind.

But of course, something always has to be there to ruin it all.

A looming shadow creeps over her shoulder. She ignores it and continues to let her eyes roam over a page in her history book. It's the same one from last week. She hasn't been able to exchange it with the library closed and all.

"Look, I'm not interested in anything you have to say." July signs and flips to the next page.

The person behind her scoffs. It's a familiar sound. One that has her suddenly sweating with panic.

July gulps deeply, her unfinished chip scratching the inside of her throat.

She twists in her seat and peers at June who looks truly sickening. She's more than sure she looked way better on the way to school than she does now. What the fuck happened within four hours?

Her sister, dressed in her cheer uniform, looks awful. Those once perky curls now lay limp and greasy atop her head. All the colors in her face have long been drained. What remains is those dark circles under her dull blue eyes and the waxy hue over her cheeks.

Shit. Her boorish eyes started to sink back into her skull, threatening to leave their sockets.

It may not be safe to say this, but she is far worse than July has ever been. Now that is wild. She better keep her mouth shut and not a say fucking word about it to her.

"Oh, what a little token loner you are. Honestly, July. This is getting so pathetic. Get a life already." June's words are intense with their croaking.

She hears a few snickers and snorts. Her eyes move away from her sister's and finds her little group of followers not too far behind with all their beaver teeth chattering with laughter.

July shrugs off her words and moves to return to her book.

A snarl leaves her sister. The sound is starling, causing her to freeze once June's hand grips her shoulder.

"I'm not done with you, you bitch." She leans close to sneer the words.

July holds her tongue. A gag tries to escape her. God, her sister's breath is horrid. Like rotting meat and sourness. Eww, her teeth are coated in a yellow film.

Her eyes go wide. She's smelled that sour stench more times than she'd like.

June tilts her head to the side in a condescending manner. "Little loner creeps like you deserve to wallow in a spoiled pool of nothingness."

Before she gets a chance to use her own words filled with hatred in retaliation something is pouring over her head, catching in her gaping mouth.

The taste of the spoiled milk in her mouth, the ruined clumps that cling to her hair spark July to stagger from the lunch table in a hurry.

Bile and her newly digesting lunch fling up her throat. She barely makes it to the nearest trashcan. Her stomach exhumes all its contents. And yet the smell of all the trash and half eaten lunch food fuels more gags out of her. She's got nothing left to release.

Their laughter sinks deep in her ears, trailing over the pink mushy parts of her mind.

Tears of sick and humiliation leak from her burning eyes.

She moves to run out of the cafeteria only to be stopped by June tripping her.

She falls onto her knees, the bones in them creaking. July groans. Embarrassment heats her cheeks. She looks and smells awful. And yet she and her sister will never be even.

Her body solidifies. Despite the spoiled milk coating her upper body like a messed-up version of a band aid, July remains on the floor. She crisscrosses her legs and lets her mind drown out their voices.

*Take deep breaths. Don't even worry about how awful you smell. Don't you fucking cry.*

Soon the final lunch bell rings and the students leave the scene. Most chuckle at her, voicing their amusement. She hears a few of their phones snap as they take pictures. More than likely, she'll be famous on Facebook by the end of the day. She'll be the talk of the town. A damn joke.

June's followers are the last to leave. They kick around her bag before filtering out into the hallway and to their next class. Acting like nothing happened. They didn't see anything of course.

Her sister crouches next to her. She refuses to meet her gaze. Not after this. Not after being ruined in more ways than she ever thought possible.

"Look at me, July. Look at me." June's words are soft and much deeper than they were earlier.

Almost like they aren't hers at all.

July sniffs and does as she says. She chokes back a gasp.

Her sister's eyes are flicking with that yellow haze. Oh, fuck.

She does her best to scramble away. June grips her ankle, greedily pulling her back toward her. Her milk-slick hands fail to get a firm grip on anything in her vicinity.

"Stop looking for a way to fix me, July. I don't want to come back. I have a purpose and you ain't gonna fuck it up for me." Her sister reveals a sinister smile, showing off those ugly yellow teeth.

But she's up close and too personal and she finally notices that June's teeth are also wickedly sharp, too unnatural of a point to be considered a freak anomaly.

July is too distracted by this discovery to see the clawed hand that whips her head to the side. June's nails sink into her flesh, dragging them across her face, letting fresh blood mix in with the soured milk.

She whimpers from the sudden burning sensation in her cheek.

After she recovers from this surprisingly hurtful hit, she finds herself to be alone in the cafeteria. June has fled. All that's left is her rumpled backpack and ruined dignity.

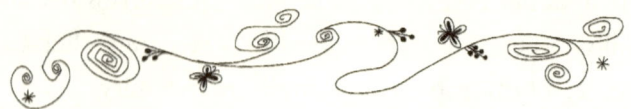

# 16. Family Breakfast

She lied to Abigail, again. It's becoming a habit. One that June usually specializes in. Never her.

July confessed that she was attacked by an angry squirrel when getting off the bus two mornings ago and landed in a nasty ditch.

It was the only thing that made any sense about the three claw marks etched into her black and blue bruised face. With her terrible timing and cruel luck, it's highly likely this will happen again.

Good thing her mother bought the lie. She didn't have the heart to tell her what happened at school. It would only have encouraged disappointment for her golden child to form within her.

Their principal pulled July into the office and begged her to tell her mother. She refused of course. No way is she getting Abigail on June's ass over nothing.

It's over. Done with. Not even relevant anymore.

The early morning sunlight crosses over the blossoming cornfield and seeps into the kitchen windows. Th rich brown cabinets glow in the sheer yellow rays.

Abigail woke them up to eat a healthy breakfast that consisted of fluffy biscuits, homemade white gravy, and wonderfully chewy bacon. So much better than the grits they've been having.

No one bothered to get any boxes of cereal the last time they went into town. Now that she's thinking about it while carefully cutting up her biscuit, she can put it on the grocery list-

Her thoughts quickly disappear the moment her nose catches a whiff of something utterly foul.

July's utensils clatter onto her plate. Her stomach groans in displeasure. The food in her belly threatens to rise in her throat after she accidentally inhales too much of the smell.

Across the kitchen island, Abigail hides a gag behind her hand. Huh, she smells it too. That's the first. This particular sour scent is only every around June and her.

She quickly turns in her chair to study her sister. Her brows rise in surprise.

Yeah, she doesn't look so good. Which has been the case for the past several days.

June's head hangs dangerously close to her plate. Nothing has been touched on it. She hasn't even used her fork to push around her soggy biscuit.

After clamping her nose shut, July slowly gets off the island stool. The moment her feet touch the ground June pitches to her left and pukes violently.

That smell grows ten times worse and has Abigail in a fit of obnoxious gags.

July barks at her to leave and that she can handle this. She fails to mention that this has happened to June before.

Their mother tosses her a freshly dampened rag before scurrying away from this grotesque scene. July doesn't blame her. She's struggling to keep her breakfast down.

But it doesn't take long for June to expel everything as she roughly pats her on the back, making sure her airways are free of that vivid yellow muck that's becoming a puddle on the floor.

She disregards the lumps of chewed biscuit that's mixed in with the yellow vomit.

July ignores the way it pulses with a flickering sheen, like it's wet and congealing. She'd find this fascinating if it weren't so bizarre.

Her sister coughs for a final time and sits back on her ankles. Her red rimmed blue eyes begin to get hazy.

She leans around her shoulder and finds her eyes struggling to become that yellow shade. As if something in June is trying to fight against it.

Oh, fuck that.

Damn. Resist it, June!

July takes the rag and wipes June's face clean. She ignores her sister's rotten breath and ruined teeth. It's nothing compared to what June must have been through those few nights ago before she got to her. She knows something bad went down. It's just impossible to know what.

It only causes her worry to flourish. The unknown is killing her sanity. But what June knows might actually be murdering her insides.

"June. What's going on with you? Please, tell me before I lose my mind." Her words seem to knock June out of the trance her sickness sunk her into.

She grins. Remnants of the vomit seep out of her yellow-stained teeth and drip down her face. July gulps and moves to clean the new mess. However, she's stopped by June, gripping her wrist so tight that she hears the bones beg to splinter in half.

Her face contorts from the pain. A sweat breaks across her forehead. And yet neither do anything to sway June to let go.

Instead, her sister leans close. Now her eyes are illuminated by this yellow that always seems to be around.

"There's no time to pay for your sins. Writhe in a cave of despair, July. You won't stop it." June headbutts her. Their noses clash into one another. Their foreheads colliding with a troublesome smack.

It jolts July into a freak out. She falls backward, hitting the tiled floor with such force that her spine cracks.

She hears June's pattering feat rush out of the kitchen. She's left alone once again. What the fuck just happened? Holy shit. June could have killed her! What stopped her from doing so?

July closes her eyes and wonders what the fuck is behind that door. There is nothing it leads to.

But what if they can't see it or at least June is the only one who can.

That encourages more questions to arise. Nothing is making sense to this.

She turns on her side, her eyes finding the door leading to the field.

Her chest squeezes. The breath in her lungs suddenly feels so cold.

There, standing right before the damn purple door is that white deer. Its face clearly getting wet from its tears.

It's a mockery of the ones that drip over the tip of her own nose. There is no need for her to be upset. And yet fear and anger swell inside her heart. Neither win over the other to take complete control. Maybe that's for the best until she gets to the bottom of this horseshit.

# 17. Gators Need To eat Too

July chose not to go out with June and their mother to find a dress for the dance. For one, it's two weeks away which leaves her plenty of time to allow Abigail to find her something simple at the thrift.

They had argued about her being able to sit this one out. Of course, their mother won, claiming this is the only chance she'll get to experience such a dance. She couldn't take her pouty lips any longer. She caved.

But also, because she's sick on the living room couch with a high fever that's resulting in the worst headaches known to man.

It seems that no matter how hard she tried to keep out of the cold it somehow got revenge on her.

Abigail fussed about her for an hour before June groaned in protest. Always the impatient one out of the two. July refrained from rolling her eyes as her sister sneered at her once walking out the front door following behind their mother like a lost duck.

She's been by herself for an hour. Boredom threatens to kill her. Her bones ache with the desire to sleep.

There is nothing new to read. All the books in her collection have been read at least three times. She can't bring herself to go for a fourth.

Well, there is the manor's study down the hall behind the staircase. She's yet to explore it and see what treasure may be hiding among the shelves lining the door. That is if there are bookshelves in the room.

Abigail said it was locked after their father was found dead in the living room. She mentioned that the key may lie within one of the kitchen island drawers.

It's too bad July doesn't have enough energy to spare to go and fetch a new book.

All there is to do is blow her nose in a continuous loop and stare at the fire that roars at the far end of the living room.

It expresses a soothing heat that wraps around her, seeping into her pajamas. A pleasant smell of burning wood clings to her as well.

Her eyes flutter close. A yawn escapes her cracked lips. This is the perfect chance to sleep and let this cold run its course.

But a faint whisper in her left ear proves irritating. She groans and pushes her face farther into the couch pillow, wishing to sink into darkness.

A sudden frosty draft whips into the living room, causing her to sink deeper beneath the fuzzy blanket she brought down from their room.

No matter how hard she clenches her eyes shut her body fails to sleep.

*Juuuuully….*

The whisper says so quietly that she almost misses it.

She jerks up on the couch. Her eyes now wider than ever as she gazes around the room. No one is here besides her. July is alone is this fucking house that she's convinced is haunted by whatever is behind the purple door.

Her chest aches from her heavy breathing. An unwanted growl rumbles in her belly. When was the last time she ate something? Ugh. The thought of food has her stomach gurgling in disgust. There might be a half drank Sprite still in the fridge. That may help-

*July!*

The voice calls again but filled with impatience. There is certainly something here with her. But what could it be? She's got the worst feeling about this.

After taking a nervous gulp to shove down the mucus stuck in the back of her throat, July turns her head around to face the entrance to the kitchen. Her heart skips the beat at the sight of what appears to be June slowly walking out of the back door.

"June?" She calls out to her, sounding unsure if it's really her. It could be the fever talking. She feels all clammy and chilled.

When the person doesn't respond July rushes to her feet a little too quickly. Her head pounds and her vison stutters even with her glasses on. Damnit, this sucks.

She stumbles a little as the blanket falls around her feet. "Shit. Wait, June!"

Too late for that. The back door slams shut before she can reach it.

July limps outside after the figure that resembles her sister too much for her liking. Her breathes are ragged as she hurries down the porch steps in search of them. She sees a dark shadow crossing through the cornfield and enter the trees.

Ignoring her trembling body, July rushes into the corn and manages to make it out on the other side with no trouble at all. That shocks her slightly. Nothing can be done about that now. No time to dwell on the ease that graces her way into the piney woods that bleeds into the swamp that leads to the neighboring state.

It's not so late in the afternoon that the sun is setting. She just wishes that it provided more heat than light. Her teeth chatter from how freezing it is. Well, that might be the cold fighting her immune system talking.

July spots a massive amount of moss on a nearby tree. It engrosses her, pulling her in its presence. Wow, this is nice. The rich green and brown colors of the tree and moss are quite pleasant.

Damnit. She shakes her head to pull herself out of this surprise fascination. Perhaps she can somehow remind herself later to go find her book about Texas wildlife and read about what grows on the native trees.

She steps back from the tree and feels her heart sink into her stomach. July has lost the dark figure that she's almost certain really isn't June. Her sister would have made sure she knew of her most glorious arrival as if she were royalty.

Her fevered mind is playing tricks on her. Nothing more to it. Hopefully. She needs to get back inside the manor before her cold turns into pneumonia or something worse.

July rubs her frigid arms. She's careful with her steps, making sure not to snap any twigs.

She takes great caution in turning around. However, her awkward grace is useless as she finds herself much deeper in the woods than she originally thought.

Her eyes are watering in panic. She tells herself not to freak out and everything will be just fine. Will it?

There's a soft trickling sound like water drops splattering in something. With no true direction to follow, July heads towards the noise. It may lead her out of this mess she created over nothing.

Crows that linger in tree branches caw in protest of her slowly weaving her way in. Chirps from toads she can't for the life of her see among the fallen leaves almost seem like a warning.

Soon she finds a small stream. She follows it in hopes of getting out. Only, she's disappointed to approach a rather large portion of the swamps.

A rotten smell drifts from the water. It's a mixture of sour soil and something along the lines of spoiled meat. July clutches her nose shut, pissed that her allergies and sickness aren't currently clogging her sinuses when she needs them to.

Willows bend low into the murky water the color of dark green. Many logs drift in the water with moss covering almost every exposed inch. Much to her own displeasure she gets closer to the bank and leans in a little.

Curiosity of this degree is dangerous. It is a danger that she sometimes, most of the time, ignores entirely.

She spots small tad poles and various minnows swimming about. Out in the distance turtle heads rise out of the water only to quickly dunk back in at the sight of her.

This is a rather satisfying area. Perhaps she can somehow convince Abigail to get someone to put a table and bench out here. It is a wonderful place to lose herself in a book.

Just as swiftly it came, all the noise in this truly spectacular ecosystem disappears in a flash. Silence now consumes this place. The hair on the back of her arms and neck stick up straight. However, it's not due to the cold that she can barely feel now on the account of her body going numb.

Before she can question the change of the atmosphere a massive alligator covered in moss surges from the muddy swamp and latches onto her right leg with its powerful jaws.

July screams in terror as well as agony. Its teeth sink into her pajama pant leg and through her flesh. It dares to shake its head, her small frame moving along with it.

"Fuck!" Her cries bounce off the trees around her, encasing July in her own fear.

Tears stream down her face. Her leg is bleeding and absolutely on fire. Any more of this and her flesh will tear off her bones. The feel of its warm breath swirling around her causes July to cry harder.

And yet there's a look in its rather devastating green-yellow eyes. It's waiting for something.

Her panicked huffs blow strands of hair sticky with sweat out of her face.

It stalls its attack long enough for something behind her to make too much noise on purpose just to fuck with her.

July peers over her shoulder with the gator still holding onto her now throbbing leg. Blood leaks over her searing skin and soaks into her ripped pajama leg, pooling around her to sink into the ground.

She briefly assumes it will be a form of June standing there waiting to offer her a smirk. Instead, she finds that dark figure formed by shadows and clouds of smoke. The same that had shown itself to her a while ago in the manor.

*"Stop this pathic search for answers. No need to spoil the surprise that will soon come upon us all."* The voice of it is deep and crackling. It irritates her eardrums.

She inhales deeply before coughing up a loogy to spit at the feet it possibly might conjure because that will show it. God, can't she for once not fight back?

It clicks its tongue. It leans in a disapproving way. She could care less about what it thinks of herself. And yet it doesn't stop the fear that swells in her chest. Any much more of this then she might piss herself.

*"Soon you will come to understand what it means to be a part of something so great. I look forward to it."* She watches it with wide eyes as it lifts a smoking hand with claw-tipped fingers. It snaps and then a rushing of her blood washes down the side of her leg.

July whips her head back and finds the gator now gone. It disappeared without a trace. There aren't even tracks from where it dragged its body along the bank to get to her. However, it left her bleeding. She hopes it enjoyed their little temporary joining.

But as she turns back around, she finds herself no longer within the swamp or woods at all. It brought her to the cornfield and perched her right before the purple door.

Taking another glance at her leg she finds the wounds already half healed and all the fresh blood from her flesh completely gone. The rest have left her pajamas stained.

She doesn't give the tears that wet her face much attention as she gets to her feet. This thing, whatever it may be, wants to mess with her. Fill her mind with tricks and unwanted fear.

She knows it's what has been causing her and June so much torment. It's what influences her.

Well, it must know this. Nothing it can do or say will encourage her to stop her hunting for answers. She must get to the bottom of this. No one else can. She won't let anyone in on this unless necessary.

July flips her middle finger at the door and slowly makes her way up the porch and into the house where the fire still burns perfectly.

# 18. Mysterious Situation

The library is still not open. It hasn't been for the past three weeks. Dust has been collecting on the door handle. Where is Ms. Tibbs?

She turns on her heal and hurries to find an empty classroom.

July needs her now more than ever. She needs to get here soon before the Senior dance and graduation. No more time should be wasted on this.

Her sister is getting worse. More agitated and sluggish than ever. The not-so-fun pranks she's been pulling have gotten crueler and terrifyingly dangerous.

As if she intends to do deadly harm to July. And that devastating yellow haze over her eyes each time her lips part to let out a sinister laugh, it's getting a bit much.

This really blows.

Even those fucking butterflies have started to follow them each morning they get on the bus for school. Some manage to filter through the cracked-open windows and linger in the air, hovering close by.

And the funny thing is they're nowhere to be found the second June steps off the bus and into the school's courtyard.

They just vanish. Poof. *Gone.*

She hasn't spotted the white deer in a while either. But she knows he is lurking about. Yes, after looking through her wildlife book she made the conclusion that the white deer is a male. One that looks rather feminine if she's being honest.

July doesn't know if she should be glad he wasn't there or be afraid of his lack of presence.

Later today she'll ask Abigail if she can be dropped off at that old creepy bookstore that she ran into Ms. Tibbs outside of.

Well, convincing her mother to take her into town doesn't take much effort at all.

Apparently, June needs to find a backup Senior dance dress in case she changes her mind on what to wear at the last minute. That's very on brand for her sister. She is more than happy not to participate more than she already has.

Plus, it gives her time to do proper investigating without the problem lurking over her shoulder.

She trips on her own two feet the second she gets out of the truck, but she still runs inside the bookshop with a wide smile on her face.

The moment she is greeted by stale air and hundreds of used books she makes a beeline for the very back. There against the far wall are a row of three community computers that have no lock on them. Anyone can get on and search till their hearts are full of content.

July sits at the one in the very corner away from prying eyes. The second her ass collides with the limp cushion of the rolling chair a waft of dust flutters straight up her nose and mouth.

She coughs till her throat grows hoarse. Then a tap on her shoulder springs her out of this sickly fit. July inhales sharply, almost too quickly for her breaths to get back under control.

Her heart lodges in her throat at the sight of thin wrinkled fingers touching her. She horridly looks up and finds the store owner offering a bottle of water.

Heat floods her cheeks and down the sides of her neck. She can feel her pulse racing beneath her skin.

July mutters a rushed thanks before accessing the computer.

Before typing anything into the generic search engine she carefully peers over her shoulder. There she spots the owner at the register speaking with a customer who holds a stack of old tomes they must have found in the historical section of the shop.

There isn't anyone else that could potentially be watching her every move.

She steadies her hands and uses slightly shaking fingers to type in a word that might confirm her insanity. Something that very well may come back to truly haunt her mind more than what's going on inside Birkstone Manor. A feeling that can certainly end whatever pureness she has left.

There is no going back now.

July types each letter on the dusty keyboard very slowly. Her heart thumps madly.

When it's finished and lingering in the search bar eagerly awaiting her to press the search button, July squirms in her chair.

Possession.

That's the word she debated about whether to classify her and June's problems.

As she thinks upon it, the possibility is very much there. Sure, it sounds insane. And yet there is nothing else that might explain it.

Her lips dip into a frown as she quickly deletes the word to be replaced with 'strange occurrences in Swamp Hill'. That seems like a more specific search to start with.

Much to her surprise, several articles written by the local newspaper pop onto the screen. She feels her heart clench after briefly skimming her eyes over the top article's name, *Mysterious Deaths in Birkstone Manor over the decades.* Well, that certainly wasn't even on her mind when she got in here.

Without thinking she clicks on the article. It takes over the screen with its oddly dark aesthetic and menacing title that had caught her eye.

As she skims through the first paragraph, she realizes something she probably should have earlier. She and her sister are the first female heirs to inherit the manor. It's been sons every generation to do this. There is some significance in that.

Of course, that has to be a connection. Why else would things get strange and deadly the moment they move in?

However, that idea quickly morphs into a completely different one.

According to this article, mysterious ritualistic items such as homemade voodoo dolls and altars filled with strange things have been found around the cornfield surrounding the manor. Some believed them to be a warning for stupid people from going into the field. Others suggest it may be the Birkstones themselves who made it all. To perhaps keep something contained.

Everything she is reading seems to circle back to an unspoken source. That damn door. A few old black and white photos that show the manor always have it lurking in the background. People from even back then have been drawn to it whether they knew it or not.

It entrances, captivating unwilling attention like a fly caught in a spider's web.

She hurries to click out of this article and goes to the one below it.

This one recalls weird deaths that have occurred in town. Most were young children who choked on their own vomit and older teens that were found dead in neighboring fields with their eyes leaking yellow muck.

Most suggested it to be some sort of food poisoning while others went in a different direction.

It quotes the town's only church preacher on the matter at the time. He claimed that it was the work of the Devil himself. The idea doesn't seem too far off.

July abandons this article to search through the rest. They all say the same. That the manor is cursed and all who get involved with it or near its land end up dead. That perhaps there are signs of a sinister force trying its best to corrupt the young and vulnerable.

Kids much like June and her. There must be a particular trait or vibe that this thing wants to exploit for its own gain. She fails to see the connection other them all being youngsters who had an apparent bad streak.

Her brows squint in frustration. It only fuels her questions about what happened to their biological father. Neither she nor June met him. Their mother wouldn't allow him to visit even if he dared to ask.

Does Abigail know something about this town? It's a good idea to ask. Why else would they have stayed away from this place for so long? It can't just be because their father didn't want anything to do with them.

Damn. That brings along a thought that never sprouted in her mind till now. He must have wanted to be in their life. It's possibly he pushed their mother away to keep her safe. Oh, if that's the reason then their father couldn't have just randomly died.

There has to be someone in this town who knew their father. She'll get an answer to that someday.

Before she can further enhance her findings, this time including the word possession into the search bar, a loud crash shouts behind her.

She whips her head around. Her braided hair slamming against her back. July hurries to keep her glasses from slipping down her face.

The shop owner is picking up a stack of magazines she must have knocked off the counter.

With a breath of relief, July clicks out of the current article. Then she clears her search history and deletes every trace of her ever being on this computer.

She fiddles in the bag she usually carries with her and fetches her inhaler. After deeply inhaling two puffs she gets on her feet.

July is nowhere near being close to discovering what the hell is going on with June and the person who might have an answer isn't even in the country.

How convenient. Just her luck.

She bids the shop owner farewell and manages to get outside and away from the swirling dust bunnies.

Her system is shocked by the drop in temperature and setting sun. She must have been in there a while because she spots her sister and mother walking down the sidewalk towards her.

She steps ahead to meet them halfway only to be halted by a woman's rather old boxer dog that she's walking next to July. It barks madly ahead of them. Its voice cracking the closer June and their mother gets.

"Shit!" July shouts as she tries to get around the dog.

It pulls against its collar, yanking its owner behind him.

"Jeez. Let's get out of here girls." Abigail moves to corral July. She stumbles a little as the tip of her foot catches in a crack in the sidewalk.

June is close enough to catch her. But her eyes flash yellow when remaining in place, letting her sister fall face first.

The dog keeps on hollowing. Its roaring cries make her ears hurt.

July screams when hearing a sharp crack fill the air. A rush of hot blood leaks from her nostrils and trails down her chin and neck. Her shirt and jacket are soon covered in it.

Abigail quickly helps her up and takes her shoulders tightly, keeping her on her feet.

They begin in the opposite direction. However, they notice that June isn't following behind. Abigail huffs loudly and turns them around.

July finds her sister crouching on her knees to snarl into the dog's face. Her mouth and nose scrunch with the action. It whimpers and scatters away from June.

She can see the fear in his clouded eyes as it scampers from June with his owner quickly after him. The intense throbbing in her nose doesn't compare to what that poor dog must be feeling. She's never seen June do anything like that before.

It must be what she looks like when tormenting July.

Well, that's going to be stopped soon. No more will she be her punching bag just for the hell of it. Fuck that.

# 19. Senior Dance

July doesn't feel quite like herself. Hell, she doesn't even look normal. All this hairspray is killing her sinuses. What's the point of having her hair curled and set in place like cement?

Her ribcage itches as if red fire ants out in the cornfield decided to hunker down in her dress. Why would someone make such a nice-looking dress with this incredibly scratchy material that sheds the worst amount of glitter every time she takes a step?

Each of her toes are squished together in the points of her small heals Abigail insisted upon her wearing. That's the only reason she's attending this stupid fucking dance.

For her precious mother who is constantly taken advantage of by her greedy daughter.

July kept her mouth shut the entire time June spent bitching at Abigail for almost frying her hair off with the curling iron. Their room is going to smell burnt for a while. And yet it was her sister's deep unnerving voice that truly acted like icing on the cake.

That was two hours ago.

They're now waiting in the living room while their mother is outside in the front to warm the truck. She may also be scraping ice off the windshield. It's hard to tell.

It sucks that their early graduation will be at the highest point of winter. They should have asked to walk across the stage with the rest of the seniors later in the spring. Too bad they came to Swamp Hill with more class credits than what was expected of them.

All she needs to do before that inevitable ceremony is to start picking which colleges to apply for. She's smart enough to get at least one full ride scholarship. Her academic record only proves her brain power.

A good reason why a lot of the kids at school snicker at her every time they catch her sneaking away to the library when it was still open.

No one likes a know-it-all anymore. Not even teachers who usually applaud quick thinking and instant knowledge.

July dwells on several possibilities as to why Ms. Tibbs hasn't come back yet when June sits next to her on the couch.

She quickly ignores the tremor of upset nerves that singe the inside of her stomach to peer at her much prettier and dangerous twin.

June ended up choosing her first dress choice to wear at this stupid dance. It's a slim style gown made from dark dusty pink fabric that hugs her hips a little too tight. She can see her sister's bones sticking out.

The bodice is sinched around her extremely thin waist, carving out her ribcage. And those tiny spaghetti straps do nothing to distract from those awfully prominent collar-bones.

None of her crisp pink makeup can hide the gloomy purple circles under her eyes. That rather expensive concealer really is failing at its one purpose.

Damn. Even her hair is fried and not just by the curling iron either. Everything about June is off and too close to death in July's opinion.

It makes her feel slightly better about herself. She may be drowning in too many yards of sparkly dark green tule but at least she has some meat on her bones. July is so very grateful that the small puffy princess sleeves that connect to the worst corset top give her faint warmth against this freezing night.

She opted out on wearing makeup or doing anything to her hair other than putting it in a long braid that fell down her back.

June catches July's heavy stare and sneers at her.

The deadly look in her heated dull blue eyes causes July to flinch away in surprise and fear all at once.

"What the fuck are you looking at?" June's voice is oddly consumed by something caught in the back of her throat as she breaks into a fit of coughs.

July cringes away, wishing she could be anywhere else but here. She wonders if the truck is warm enough to get in.

"N-Nothing at all, June." Without meaning to she aims her troubles gaze to her ugly brown heels that their mother found in the thrift store along with her dress.

She hears her sister chuckle darkly. The couch dips in as June leans close to whisper in her ear. "I'm sorry for snapping at you. Forgive me?"

Sorry? As in an apology? Words like that have never fled her prink glossed lips ever in their entire lives. At least not with meaning.

Those tricky words act like a pinball machine inside her chest. She clutches the edge of the couch cushion and grips it for dear life.

"Do you hear me, July? I'm really sorry for being such a jerk lately. I didn't even mean to hit you those last few times. It just came out of me." June continues with her apology.

There isn't much she can do other than gawk at her sister like a fish out of the nearest lake clinging to its last crippling breath.

July can't even fathom anything to say. Shock gulps her up, enveloping her like a sticky fly trap. This can't be real. It doesn't feel right.

"The whole spoiled milk thing was truly cruel, and it wasn't supposed to go that far. I meant to offer it to you as a prank, but it turned into something worse. It's like I was an entirely different person that day. Please, you have to believe me, July." June is speaking to her, doing so much as to take hold of her shaking hands, intertwining their fingers like they did when they were kids.

It feels utterly wrong.

And yet the way her sister fights back the tears that linger in her glassy eyes is telling her something different.

Perhaps the wrongness that she feels is disbelief. Yes. That makes sense.

She clears her throat and attempts tugging her hands away from June. However, her sister only tightens her hold on July and urges her to say something with a small smile.

"I appreciate the apology, June." This doesn't mean she accepts any words that come out of her sister's mouth.

She may be in her sort of right mind now but most of those times she wasn't anything like herself at all. Whatever lingers beyond the purple door is using her for something.

At this point she doesn't care about what it may be. She wants to know why. What is the purpose of it?

June jumps on the couch a little. Her smile only widens. July watches as she takes her hands back to wipe the few tears dripping down her cheeks that are covered in an insane amount of blush.

"Good because I have a surprise waiting for you outside in the cornfield." She almost shouts this in a spasm of glee. "Hurry before he freezes to death!"

Her brows squint in suspicion. "He? Who's out there?"

June rolls her eyes and gently takes her elbow to help her off the couch. She doesn't say a word when tossing her jacket to her. Well, this should be interesting.

Her sister says nothing as she too bundles up and leads her to the back door.

The sun is slowly descending behind the tree line, disappearing to welcome the chilling night. It'd be wonderful if snow started to fall from the gloomy clouds that linger above them. Too bad it never snows here.

"C'mon already." June whisper shouts to keep the surprise hidden.

She rolls her eyes and follows her, careful as to how she steps down from the marble porch that's way too slick for her liking. Her heart jumps to her throat as she just barely catches herself onto the nearest column when her heel slips on the very bottom step.

July gulps down her sudden fear and allows the warm feeling of sisterly comfort to take over.

The motion lights that Abigail had a local company come out to install quickly do their best to illuminate the corn. It fails to brighten the center of the field with how far away the lamps are positioned.

It's no matter. She doesn't really need to see with June keeping her close.

They arrive before the purple door after weaving through the frozen corn for almost ten minutes. Surely their mother is back inside the manor and now looking for them.

She squints into the darkness. There isn't enough light to see properly. And of course, having her already troubled vision doesn't do her any good.

"There isn't anyone here." She shakes her head as disappointment settles in her cold bones.

It's no surprise that June would lead her out here for absolutely nothing. She can't help but wonder what joke she's playing on her this time.

As her sister steps away from her she frowns deeply. There is something out here waiting for her alright. She's more terrified that she has no clue what it is.

"No, he's out here. I can assure you that Eli Harker wouldn't stand up a girl. Especially not one as mentally gifted as you." June brings her hands close together above her chest.

She would have noted that June isn't wearing any coat at all if it wasn't for the confusion that now laces her thoughts.

Eli Harker is one of the three football captains in their school. He's known to sometimes hang around June and her crew of the worst people imaginable. The token school bullies who never have anything better to do than pick on people.

That doesn't explain why Eli Harker is out here. Especially for someone like July.

She shakes her head as a rabid flush attack her cheeks. Her body's way of trying to keep her warm. Actually, it may be a flash of embarrassment. It's hard to tell out here.

June shakes her head as she tries to hide that familiar smirk. She's up to something. Damn, she should have known better than to follow her out into the growing night.

The temperature keeps dropping every few minutes. Too long of a time to be out here. She hates the way her teeth are chattering, scraping against each other.

"Look, he's been eyeing you since we got to this school. He's even told me how cute he thinks you are. It's a shame he was too nervous to ask you to the dance. I managed to convince him to come and take you to the dance anyway. Are you angry with me?" She receives a pouting lip from her sister.

Should she embrace this or question it further? July fails to decide.

Well, come to think of it, Eli Harker is quite nice looking with his black curls and vibrant green eyes. Most of the girls giggle over him each time he passes them in the halls. Teachers brag about his interesting smarts.

But he's been looking at July?

No. That doesn't seem right at all. If anything, it's one of her worst nightmares. July hates any type of attention. This must be a joke.

And yet June is doing everything to convince her otherwise.

Instead of trying to figure out the root of this odd gesture courtesy of June, she squares her shoulders and inhales a deep breath that coats her esophagus with a sinister chill.

She opens her mouth to say how kind her sister is only to clamp it shut at the sight of June's grin. Shit. Of course, she should have trusted her guts that said this wasn't real.

Laughter that influences fear sparks into the darkening night. It comes from June before she puts her fingers into her mouth to whistle loudly.

July is quick to cover her ears, temporarily relieving her eardrums of the sharp noise. Much to her pleasure, June stops in time for strange figures to walk out of the corn and into the middle of the field.

They're all a part of June's friend group. She recognizes her new best friend Trudy, the cheerleader. Each of them carries a wicked smile on their faces. Being dressed in their finest gowns and tuxes reveals that they have been planning this since the dance was announced weeks ago.

It's enough for her heart to jump, skipping beats that cause her chest to grow an ache.

There is no Eli Harker among them. She should have known better.

June is highly aware of the drooping of her frown. "Eli asked Shelly Williams to the dance last week. He's already picked her up. Right now, they're in each other's arms swaying to the first few songs of the dance. I'm not sorry to disappoint."

The information isn't what makes her upset. It's the fact that she almost believed that June was sorry for all of it. She won't fall for it again.

"Whatever." She tries to play off her disappointment that rushes through her cold veins.

Her sister shrugs and uses her hands to give her friends some type of signal that she fails to find any true meaning for.

They all nod their heads and reveal their hands which were all uniformed and placed behind their backs.

July staggers backward at the sight of rotten tomatoes and apples in their hands.

"I managed to bribe a cafeteria lady for some rotten things. There is much better use for them instead of decomposing in a garden waste bin. Care to guess what that might be, July? Oh, don't give me that look. You are going to love it." She says after July grimaces when hearing one of them dig their fingers into a soggy apple.

It makes the worst squelching sound. Her stomach flips as they all take exactly three steps towards her with their hands filled with rotten fruits now aimed at her.

She shakes her head profusely as June takes a spare tomato with the worst dark spots that a girl wearing the ugliest yellow short dress hands her.

"Don't worry. We'll try not to throw them at your face. Though, I make no promises." She shoots July one last smirk before clicking her tongue.

The final signal for them is to abide by. There is no time for her to cower behind the purple door. One by one they toss the food at her, hitting her arms and chest like the most awful smelling boulders.

A pathetic whimper escapes her mouth when a stray apple hits her right in the jaw. It collides with her neck and almost instantly melts against her freezing flesh. The nasty gunk seeps into her jacket.

The force of each hit brings her further to the ground that's still moist from this morning's dew.

Their heinous cackles and fun-filled hollers are almost enough to drive her insane.

When there's nothing left to ruin her with, they pat June on the back. Congratulating her on the best prank of the century. None even bother to check on her as she withers on the ground with the engulfing mud staining her dress.

She can't look her sister in the eye. Hatred for her and self-loathing swarm around in her quaking stomach, doing their best to eat her from the inside.

The long minutes drag slowly enough to where she doesn't realize that June has left her to her lonesome to catch up with her weird followers.

Neither does she find enough courage to get up on her feet to stumble back into the house to take a shower. She should. Everything about her now smells like a pig trough filled with muck.

Oh, how the Devil must be grinning at her. The ultimate sucker. It seems like a fitting title for her.

A while later, after her fingers threaten to grasp onto a form of frostbite, she hears the back door open in a hurry. The slam of it hitting the outer wall has July jolting. And yet she doesn't have the heart to look at her mother who must be wondering why the fuck she's all this time been out here.

"Hey, June's friends came by to pick her up for the dance. C'mon, you're already late." Abigail skips out of the house with an annoying pitch to her voice.

*Well, it's a tough one to explain. You certainly won't believe me this time, mother.*

Her thoughts are scrambled. She fails to hear what Abigail is saying when lifting her up and out of the dirt.

She sleeps alone in their room. There's a dark voice throughout the night. It's an unsettling tone that seems to resonate with the door far out in the middle of the field where her last wave of humiliation occurred.

July knows it's connected somehow. It whispers the vilest things. Some of them can't wound her like June has. And yet it doesn't stop even when she clenches her eyes shut and hides under her many blankets.

She ignores its call. Refusing to accept the darkness it brings. Judging by the smell that infiltrates the room and creaking doors in the hallway, it doesn't appreciate her rejection of it.

## 20. You Called?

Abigail wanted to take June and July out to a nice dinner in town to celebrate their upcoming graduation. July made the excuse of not feeling well to get out of it. June scowled at her every chance that presented itself.

Her twin didn't walk out of the house without kicking her in the knee at least twice. It's a good thing their mother had already gone to the truck. That would've been an interesting argument.

Not wanting to venture up the stairs with a now throbbing right knee, she takes an unfinished book to the couch with her and snuggles under a blanket.

She forgot to ask their mother to fix the fireplace before she left. July can only hope that the manor's finicky heating system can make this a little cozier.

July flips through the pages of a random romance novel. Not her usual choice but it was at the top of the stack that sits on her dresser. She wasn't paying any real attention to what she picked up on the way out of the room.

Her mind struggles to find any of the characters appealing. But the ringing blasting from the landline saves the day.

With a soft grunt she tosses the book onto the couch and gets up to answer the phone.

It keeps ringing as she reaches it. "Jeez."

She holds the phone with two hands up to her ear. Her eyes aim at the opposite wall that is made up of some of the cabinets.

"Hello?" She sighs into the bottom of the phone.

All that responds is static. There's nothing on the other end. Something must be wrong with the damn thing. She huffs while angrily putting it back onto the wall.

Maybe she isn't so grateful to have been interrupted while only three chapters into her book.

July makes it halfway into the living room when the phone rings again. She rolls her eyes and races to answer it, nearly colliding with the back of the couch in the process.

"Yes?" This time she speaks with more sternness than necessary.

One of the lights flicker in the kitchen. She pauses, moving the phone away from her ear. "Hello?" She calls out.

There's no way her mother and sister are back yet. They left thirty minutes ago. And despite June acting off she will always take her time enjoying a meal. That's just June. The prissy cheerleader every boy wants to be with, and every girl wants to be.

No one in the house answers her so she gets back to the phone. Along with the static noise, it is faint crackling. Is that heavy breathing on the other end of the line?

"June, if you found a payphone just to fuck with me, cut it out. It's not funny." She brings the bottom of the phone closer to her mouth to hiss the words.

However, her body is quickly consumed by a dowsing of fear. This isn't right.

"Please, leave me alone till y'all get home." Her voice is submerged in a pleading tone. She desperately hopes June will willingly comply. She's had enough of her pranks to last a lifetime.

*"July? Juully… Juuuulllyyyy!"* A deep voice filled with crackles shouts into the phone loudly. The words slam into her ears, forcing her to drop the phone and let it hang by the cord as she hurriedly backs way.

Her heart bangs within her chest as she rushes into the living room. There she finds all the lights she kept on flickering. Shadows from the taxidermy decorating the walls spread across the room. It's a madhouse here.

Strange shouts and screams echo from up the stairs down to her. Heavy footsteps come from up the stairs. Oh, shit.

July gives a frightened cry and abandons her book and the decently plush couch. Her feet don't stop moving until she reaches the back porch. Even then she keeps going far into the cornstalks. Ultimately leading herself to the purple door.

All of what just occurred must be its doing. There is no explanation.

She swallows thickly, fighting against the lump in her throat.

The air is cold. The later afternoon light is warm, however. Both cancel each other out.

July struggles to keep standing as the white deer reveals itself, staggering into the center of the field. He won't approach the door. All he can do is offer her a sharp whimper. She grows angry while watching his tears. Who does he think he is to feel anything for her?

That anger acts like fuel. Giving her permission to lash her thoughts at him.

"Why do you get to cry while you stand there and watch this happen? Don't you have some kind of power to get rid of all this shit? Damnit, help me. Do something!" July shouts at it. Her hands waving in the air furiously.

The monarch butterflies that linger in the cornstalks flutter their wings at her rash tone. Well, fuck them too.

Muddled voices enter her mind. They do their best to brush up on her thoughts, wanting to infiltrate her memories. It's that fucking door doing this.

She turns her attention to the purple door and growls at it. Frustration lingers in her body, willing her to act in such a way knowing that whatever it really is does have the power to do something awful.

July looks at the deer once more. It's taken a few steps backward, gaining more distance from her and the door.

"Fuck you and these damn butterflies. I don't need your help anyway." She can't determine if that's a lie or not. July doesn't have a clue as to what this deer can do. It's offered nothing in terms of aid or information.

Shit. Does she expect this pale beast to talk? Of course not. But wishing it could doesn't hurt.

She spits in the deer's direction. It's a vulgar gesture and all she has in her current personal arsenal.

July disregards the possibility of something waiting for her inside and storms up the porch. It's easy to dismiss the pain in her knee. Not like she hasn't felt it before.

# 21. Fear

Kids at Swamp Hill High School think it's enjoyable to hang out in the school parking lot after the final bell for reasons that she fails to understand. There is no appeal to it according to July.

The dance was days ago and now the after-school parking lot is buzzing with girls exchanging photos and guys talking about which ones got laid in the only motel in town while the others stood guard at the door.

They are all jittery bees who seem to be lacking a queen to keep them in line.

Yes, she's talking about her twin sister June.

She's been standing outside of the double back doors where the very few buses usually stop to pick the kids up. There has been no sign of June at all.

This isn't unusual. Her sister has been disappearing more and more lately. Neither she nor their mother can figure out where she goes. And by the looks of her little bullying squad who are currently lingering around their rusty cars and massive trucks, she hasn't been with them either.

Damnit. She missed the bus because she decided to wait for June. Once again it was a bad idea.

July will have to go back through the front of the school to reach the main office and ask to call home. Abigail is going to be pissed.

With a roll of her eyes, she tucks her scratchy blue and red scarf tighter around her neck to fight against the stubborn cold that's been refusing to leave. Soon it will be spring. It needs to arrive in Swamp Hill fast.

She huffs when almost slipping off the curb to cut around the side of the school.

But of course, luck is never on her side. July is stopped by a shout of her name that came from behind her. She sighs heavily and mentally prepares for someone with enough balls to come up and say something mean or toss a used nose tissue at her.

It's happened a surprising four times since arriving in town. She really doesn't want a fifth time. The last one was filled with infected green snot that got all in her mouth. She has no desire to catch the flu again.

"Hey, can we talk to you?" She turns around to find every single person who tossed ruined food at her those few nights ago standing before her looking so fucking guilty. Trudy is among them twirling her bright blonde hair and avoids looking her in the eyes.

Huh. Isn't that hilarious? She, however, doesn't find any of their watering eyes or self-inflicted frowns funny.

The tall guy standing in the middle wearing a letterman jacket with the most patches she's ever seen rubs the back of his neck. His shoulder length brown hair blows in the breeze. He was the one to stop her. She can't remember if his name is Bruce or Matt.

She could have already called Abigail by now. What a waste of her time.

"Look, we took that too far." A short girl with pale blonde hair and dark freckles covering her brightly tinted pink cheeks huffs. Her eyes flickering to Trudy, waiting for the other girl to say something.

She won't. Not willingly. That is her sister's most loyal follower.

July notices the way the girl grips the letterman jacket guy's elbow. What's her name? It might be Terra. She isn't too sure.

Oh, what the hell, their names don't matter to her at all.

"Took what too far?" July tilts her head, aiming her heated gaze at the girl.

It may be a stupid idea to lock eyes with someone very capable of harm. Whether that be throwing squishy browned tomatoes at her or tripping her in the halls. But no one is as evil as June Birkstone.

The other girl standing on the opposite side of letterman guy snickers. The sound is consumed by a rage that still manages to linger despite June's absence.

"June convinced us to hand her our college application letters. She said she would take all of them to the post office when she got done filling out hers. But then she held them hostage until we went along with her stupid plan to keep you from going to the dance." She explains in a raspy voice that pairs well with her black eyeliner and choppy dark brown hair.

"She's been doing things like that for a while now. We have no idea why." The other guy standing to their far left shrugs his shoulders. The leather jacket he wears crinkles and reflects the afternoon sun.

July rolls her eyes again and refuses to believe a word. But that does sound like the person who her sister is becoming. However, it's worse that other people are starting to notice it too.

This is bad. This is very bad.

"We weren't like this before y'all got to town." Short blondie stomps her feet and causes her frilly cardigan to flutter.

Trudy bites her top lip and gives a slight nod.

Wow. They want to apologize but fail to understand that she's been going through this her entire life. They just don't get it. No one ever does. She doesn't need nor want their fucking pity. They can rot in their own guilt for all she cares.

Without thinking she drops her bag to the ground and points a finger at all of them. This instantly grasps their attention. All of them cringe at her crooked pointer finger that she broke in the fifth grade after falling off a bike.

She vividly remembers June standing there, refusing to help her off the ground, cackling like a witch. Abigail never let July ride one again.

"Alright you assholes. June is the pink sparkly cheerleader and I'm the typical sickly kid that gets bullied by said cheerleader. That's how it's been since the dawn of our time on this fucking planet. I'm so damn sorry you're just now seeing through her perfect white smile and bouncy blonde hair. Now, why don't y'all leave me alone and never talk to me again?" Her chest rises and falls rapidly. Her lungs are on fire.

She's never talked so fast in her life. But it needed to be said. They have to hear it or else they won't ever find a chance to get away from her sister.

They may be bullies but no one deserves to be under June's wing.

"June quit the cheer team weeks ago. She hasn't been hanging out with us for a while either. We have no clue where she goes off too. It's fucking crazy." Leather jacket guy confesses.

This new information shouldn't be surprising. And yet she hadn't thought of June also abandoning her so-called friends either. In a weird way she's always been loyal to her followers who unknowingly act like her pet at times.

Instead of further bashing her sister to somehow get her friends to continue exposing her strange new habits, July bites her tongue and offers them a kind smile. Though it appears more like a grimace.

She's doing her best to build a peaceful bridge, damnit.

She pushes up her glasses and retrieves her bag off the ground.

"Look, I think she's having a rough time being here in Swamp Hill. The father that had never been around suddenly died and gifts us his big ass mansion in the middle of the woods is quite the spectacle. I'm sure she'll come around and start acting like herself again. Please, if you see her anywhere, don't hesitate to reach out and offer your support. She needs it more than I do." The lies that spill from her tongue are so damn bitter.

July struggles to keep from bursting out into fits of giggles. This has got to be the worst way to approach her school bullies who practically worship her sister.

It had to be done. No need for them to grow curious and hunt June down in order to get answers to whatever pathetic questions they may have. If she doesn't already have that luxury then neither will they.

Their early graduation is in a few days, which doesn't give her much leeway to discover June's awful secrets and barbaric behavior. Plus, she really wants to get rid of whatever is haunting her in Birkstone Manor.

It hasn't left her alone and keeps getting worse. She fears that if something else happens then there's no telling if she can remain sane.

She bids them farewell and hurries around the school, cutting through the main parking lot to gain access to the road. It will lead her straight through town and eventually to the manor.

There's no need to wait on Abigail to fetch her. She's in the worst fucking hurry of her bruised and battered life.

Before she could make it to the open road the school principal ran out and shouted that Abigail was already on her way. July gave a reluctant groan and plopped down on the curb to wait for her mother. She regrets not leaving sooner.

It's better to walk in this cold. Sitting and doing nothing only lets it consume her already frail being.

However, her self-induced silence is interrupted when she hears footsteps approaching her, their feet crunching over the parking lot gravel.

Her eyes widen at the sight of a decently put together Chuck getting closer to her. Guilt rams into her chest as she staggers upward, almost falling backward with the quick motion.

She quickly takes note of his freshly dyed hair. Pure black that shines a little blue in the dying sunlight. Her lungs clench tight.

Before she can say a word he gently smiles at her. "Look, I wanted to thank you for getting me away from her. I knew she wanted to get freaky in the shed but I didn't realize how messed up she really was. I asked for it."

July scoffs, instantly hating him trying to take accountability for how June completely took control over him. She sniffs harshly with a grimace.

"Don't blame yourself for what she did. Don't ever think it was your fault for her assaulting you. There is no fucking excuse for it. I can't even apologize on either of our behalf. But know one thing. June is unwell and I plan to put a stop to it and to her disgusting ways." July can't control the tears that slip from her face. They quickly begin to freeze on her cheeks, branding her with further guilt and anger mixed in.

Chuck shrugs, bringing his dark gray sweater tighter around himself. She hates the look of his slowly healing bottom lip. June tore it in multiple places. Her guts twist terribly tight, forcing her to grit her teeth.

"Yeah, I guess you're right." Chuck sighs and begins to turn away. July hears a truck getting closer down the road. Abigail is almost here.

Then Chuck gives her one last smile. She doesn't deserve it.

"I know June isn't actually on drugs. This town is different from others. Filled with stories not many people can understand. I hope you can help her out before it gets worse." He leaves her alone with her thoughts.

Abigail hollers for her after lowering the passenger window. July swallows down the frustrated shout that was simmering in her throat and gets into the truck.

Not only does she need to get to the bottom of this for her sister but also for her various victims that July wasn't able to help. Because she knows that her twin is more than teenage girl evil.

## 22. evil

F inally. Whatever bird or small animal that's been chirping nonstop during the night has ceased its noise. July
gladly sighs in relief. Perhaps her migraine will dissipate in a
while.

She slowly rolls on her side in her bed that is very warm due
to her body heat. It's a shame that she must leave its comfort
and act out her plan before she runs out of time.

There's a feeling in her guts. A warning that swells in her
belly that won't let up. It's been there for a few days now.
But this morning it's much worse. The only way to stop it is
to talk with Ms. Tibbs and get to the cause of June's erratic
behavior.

July carefully leans over the edge of the bed to fetch her
glasses off the side table. The small digital clock next to her

glasses says it's only a little after five. Damn. She woke up before the sun was supposed to rise.

It takes grand effort to be as silent as a mouse. However, any faint noise she may make is overpowered by the snores of her sister. She takes occasional glances at her to make sure she hasn't moved.

A stack of clothes she picked out last night sits on top of her dresser. July hurries to discard her pajamas and put the pair of dark jeans on as well as her rather fuzzy dark blue sweater. She doesn't bother to do anything with her hair. She can tell that the outside is freezing from the cold floors. Her hair being kept down will offer some warmth for her ears.

She ties the laces of her Vans tight and makes triple knots in them.

Something wild is going to happen today. She can feel it manifesting around her. Well, maybe it's that strange scratchy feeling she gets when getting closer to June's side of the room.

Smothered by the darkness swirling in the room, July fetches her sacred flashlight and switches it to the lowest setting. Without much thought she casts it across the room directly over a deep sleeping June.

July is quick to clamp her mouth shut to conceal a sorrowful whimper.

This is worse than it ever has been. She can't explain why this happens. She was almost certain that she plucked all the new weeds last night after June closed her eyes.

Covering the walls are hundreds of ivy vines. Different types of weeds and ugly flowers that lack any real color besides brown and black have completely destroyed the wood floor. Most are leaking that ugly yellow sludge. That's where the new wave of pungent sour smell is coming from.

She keeps her mouth shut to hide a gag. It stings her eyes like burning needles. The atmosphere is prickled with something on the edge of darkness. And her sister is sleeping like nothing is happening.

Taking a big risk, she takes a few steps forward to direct the light onto June.

It's so much worse than she could have ever imagined. God, she looks utterly awful.

Her skin has begun to turn into a sickly yellow. The bags under her eyes are deep purple and have little red veins leading from them. Parts of her face and neck have the worst open wounds that leak puss and once again that yellow stuff. Her sister it truly ruined.

July wipes her fresh tears away before turning away from June.

She faintly rushes down the stairs. None of the kitchen or living room lights are on. But the newly rising sun has soft orange light filling the place, unknowingly illuminating the taxidermy animals, giving them horrifying shadows that seem to follow her. They reach for her and fail to get a grasp on her.

Fogs of her hot breath collide with her face as she hurries to get to the landline. Her fingers tremble while dialing the librarian's number. She found it a while ago written in a book she hasn't been able to return due to it being closed.

The heart in her chest sputters in anticipation.

July keeps a lookout over her shoulder. Her eyes never leave the stairs. Not even as the other end of the line picks up and greets her with a groggy voice filled with sleep.

"Hello? Yes, it's me. Look, I need your help. Something is happening to June, to Birkstone Manor and you know what it is. You've just got to." There is a wobble with her voice.

For weeks she's been experiencing this all alone with no one to help her. She needs to fight against this. No one else will.

"Okay. Yes. I'll be there right when it opens. Hurry." She ends the call and quickly finds a pen and sticky notes in the junk drawer in the kitchen.

July writes to Abigail that she borrowed the car for today and not to panic. She's more than capable of driving.

As she finishes dotting and crossing her letters, she can't help but feel guilty. It doesn't last long when a striking flash of fear takes it over. Something is going to happen soon. She may not survive if she's going to be forced to finally confront June for a last time.

Damnit. She can never catch a fucking break.

She drives slowly. Her eyes never shift from the road. When they do it is to check all the mirrors and make sure she isn't accidentally stopping traffic.

It takes more effort to park the truck in the lot than it was to stir the wheel.

July cringes as she manages to squeal the brakes. Now she can guess why Abigail never wanted her to drive. Well, desperate times call for desperate measures. She's sure her mother will come to understand some day.

If she makes it out of this nightmare alive, that is.

The morning cold wraps around her, soaking through her sweater.

She gulps down a bundle of nerves that threaten to bunch in her throat. July feels eyes on her as she walks along the sidewalk. This is perhaps the first time she's been watched in secret.

Most people don't try hiding their heated gazes. If they did, then they wouldn't be able to laugh in her face about her ridiculous limp and unprovoked sneezes that come out of nowhere. Damn these allergies.

Feeling an annoying itch at the back of her head, July casually peers over her shoulder. Her eyes grow wide at the sight of a man dressed in a torn green flannel and old baseball cap quickly hide behind a lamppost.

Yes. She's been watched and worse. Followed.

She rolls her shoulders and continues. But she soon spots a woman with stringy yellow hair and a pathetic puffer jacket intently watching her from behind the glass of a butcher shop.

Oh, fuck.

July wastes no time in lightly jogging. She's careful to watch for any cracks in the concrete. Her eyes never try to search for those watching her, studying her next move. She can't afford to be distracted even with their grotesque feeling of attention.

Within a few minutes she reaches the bookstore and hurries inside. She closes the door behind her and peers out of the glass.

At least ten people who look like they crawled out of the woods stare her down. Their eyes clouded with a dark sheen perhaps conjured from determination and patience. All of them in a neat row on the opposite side of the street. Damn, this sucks. It looks like they know something's coming too.

But they are the ones who look like they will get the better end of it. Whatever it is.

She gives a startled yep as a hand grasps her shoulder. July spins around, her hands fisted and ready to hit someone.

The sight of Ms. Tibbs appearing frighted for her has July sighing in relief.

She doesn't bother giving these strange people outside any more of her attention.

"I saw you coming down the sidewalk. They're watching. We must not waste any more time. Come." The librarian leads her to the very back of the store to the couches.

The second she sits down she hears a sharp click. She whips her head around to see the store owner lock the doors. The older woman peers back at her and gives her a wink.

Well, that's somewhat reassuring. At least some people are on her side or willing to give her aid.

She turns back to Ms. Tibbs and notices her holding an old thick book with its cover made from ancient brown leather. It has different angles of stitching to keep it together. From what she can tell the tan paper has definitely seen terrible days.

"The purple door is there for a reason." Ms. Tibbs says rather darkly.

July sniffles, somewhat inhaling snot that started to trail out of her nostril. "And what reason might that be?"

The librarian shakes her head slowly. She watches the woman's brown hair glide over her shoulders that are covered in a black shawl. Why does she look like she's going to a funeral?

She shakes her head to get herself back to the point of this.

"The door is meant to keep *evil* at bay. Your sister is the key to release Him." Ms. Tibbs confesses.

July's jaw drops wide open. If she doesn't close it soon it's possible that big ass horse flies might call her mouth home.

"Strange noises and nasty smells have been haunting me. My sister is waking up in front of the door but other than that I am the only one seeing everything else. None of that makes sense. W-what are you talking about?" July wants to so badly believe that there's a logical explanation.

To convince herself that maybe all of it is in her head and that June is simply going through some normal teenage shit. Yeah. That has got to be it. No way is Birkstone Manor actually fucking haunted. She desperately wants to refuse that possibility.

And yet as she sits here in a wave of sudden silence she wonders if there is a reason why she only experienced all of this.

Ms. Tibbs clears her throat to rock July back into the present and out of her jumbled thoughts.

"I'm going to tell you all that I know. Maybe something within this dark deadly story may help you keep safe because it's too late for your sister." She says as a matter of fact.

July shrugs her shoulders and pathetically whines.

Her entire body alight with frustration and fear.

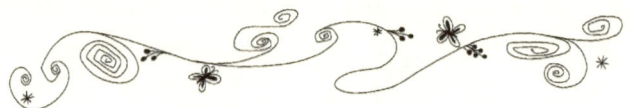

# 23. Lore

"Settlers of Swamp Hill first discovered the purple door many years ago. Way before the town got its name due to the dwelling swamp that melts with the piney woods. Anyway, those who were more susceptible to the darkness of it heard His call and pleas to get out." Ms. Tibbs begins.

July takes off her shoes and gets comfortable on the couch so her mind can fully embrace the words.

She nods her head to urge her only friend to continue. This is the most important lesson of her life. No class or lecture can compare to what is about it be revealed to her.

"As the town was coming together over the years His growing followers did everything in their power to open the door. None of their mortal tools and explosives worked. The door was indestructible. The ones more than willing to tap into the mystic arts used whatever spells they could to get the dammed thing open. None of it worked until He expressed another way. A more sinister plan to get Him out into the world." She caresses the book cover in a slow rhythm.

July watches her drag her fingertips across the stitched made from a thick red thread.

She bites the inside of her lips and suppresses a shudder. "What did this thing want them to do?"

Ms. Tibbs gives her a look full of pity. She ignores it. Never has she needed those sad eyes. They only fuel her inner rage towards the world. July is capable of being on her own even with her crazy allergies, frequent emergency room visits, and pathetic limp.

She wishes more people can see past her flaws. July is stronger than she appears.

"This *evil*, He has just enough power lingering on the other side of the door to corrupt a broken soul and use them for His bidding. That possessed person must sacrifice an innocent person before the door on the night of a blue moon. The act of such violence will trigger magic by keeping the door locked and it will finally open. Then *evil* will be free." She leans back onto the couch and hands July the book.

It feels heavy in her hands and oddly warm. Upon closer inspection she realizes this leather is actually something more disgusting. Human skin. She doesn't want to know who made this thing or whose skin this once was.

She'd like to keep down the protein bar she found in the glove box of the truck. It's only just begun to digest.

"A little a while later their attempts of this began. However, every single time they managed to set up the sacrifice something went wrong, and the possessed body gave up. Dead from the evil magic that ruined it. Soon the white deer and hordes of butterflies appeared. That's when this little cult named themselves Dead Fawn. A little 'fuck you' to God who they assumed trapped *evil* in His prison. But I'm sure you'll think otherwise after looking in that book.

"I've no idea why He chose June to be the conduit of His power or the reason He will escape. But I do know that you may be the only one to stop *evil* and His plan to destroy those who imprisoned Him in the first place." As she speaks those words something snaps inside July.

All her thoughts and fears become one as she realizes the most important detail of this.

"Oh, shit. He… This *evil* possessed June all those nights ago. I woke up and she had found her way back to bed without my help. I knew something was wrong." Tears swell in her eyes.

She doesn't instantly stop them from dripping down her face. Her shaky hands carefully take off her glass to wipe her face.

"Fuck. She may have been born a bitch, but it explains why she's the absolute worse as of recently." She mutters to herself.

The sleepwalking, sudden sickness, noises and smells were all indicators not for June but for her. Of course, *evil* was warning her of what's to come. Taunting her because He can. Telling her that there is nothing she can do to stop it.

Huh. Ain't that a bitch? She should have come to Ms. Tibbs earlier instead of waiting for her to come back to school and open the damn library.

"Once your sister performs the ritual her body will turn into its final form and ready itself to welcome *evil's* power, making Him capable of the most horrific torture you can't even begin to imagine." She confesses and points to the old book in July's hands.

"How can I stop it?" Her voice trembles and so does her heart.

"I fear that tomorrow night is the blue moon. There isn't much time left. Read the book. Dead Fawn will stop at nothing to ensure this ritual is complete. They have been waiting a long time to properly worship *evil*." Ms. Tibbs stands, ready to leave July all on her own.

The much younger girl hurries to her feet and rushes to stop the librarian.

Her eyes are red and rimmed with tears that won't stop falling. She doesn't give two shits how ugly and sad she looks.

"If what you say is true then I don't have any fucking time to read every single word in this book. Tell me, what do I need to do to save June's soul?" July holds the book tightly to her chest, afraid that all the information in it will be ripped away from her before she gets the chance to explore it.

Ms. Tibbs attempts to hold her shoulders. She pulls back. A sneer having found a way onto her face. Anger pushes back against the frightened butterflies that flutter in her stomach.

She doesn't want nor need the comfort Ms. Tibbs wants to give.

The older woman shakes her head. She trips over her own words, further delaying July's journey home.

By the troubling look on the woman's face July knows that what she is going to reveal with utterly shatter her.

# 24. And So It Begins

July stands like a rigid plank and fists clench around the book made from human skin.

"The possessed soul must be killed before the blue moon meets its highest peak." Ms. Tibbs cries as she says this. As if she knows firsthand what this information feels like and looks like as it plays out.

She scoffs. Disbelief tries to influence her. July shoves it away and squares her shoulders in response.

Her feet act quick, and she goes off to the front door when Ms. Tibbs calls out for her.

July ignores her pleas and begs for her to understand why she didn't say anything earlier. It doesn't matter now.

Followers within Dead Fawn are still outside and have doubled in numbers. No one else is on the streets. Almost like the entire town is in on this fucked up secret and has the better idea to stay hidden.

She should do the same. Perhaps even ignore what her sister plans to do tomorrow night just days before their early graduation. Well, good thing she really hates to listen to people's advice. July was always meant to be on her own. This simply proves it.

There's more to her life than listening to warnings from doctors not to be too rambunctious or to overdo it in gym class. Such as walking straight through this oddly uniformed line of Dead fawn.

July pushes between them. Her shoulders nag onto theirs, conveniently hindering her progress around them. But they don't reach out and grab her to hinder her from screwing up their plans.

Before getting out of their way completely someone clears their throat behind her. Fucking fantastic. Now what?

She turns around with a huff after stumbling to the open space on the sidewalk opposite the bookstore.

Who she finds standing there all alone puzzles her greatly. Her brows furrow in confusion. Where did they go? No one else is standing here but them. Those stalker freaks were just here.

*You're losing it, July. Keep it the fuck together.*

Instead of overshowing her panic, July casually shoves the book underneath the back of her sweater hoping the handsome man doesn't notice.

He's tall and maybe around the same age as July. Perhaps a few years older due to the frown lines that start to blend with his pale complexion that looks all the creamier paired with his long inky black hair. His eyes are quite pretty too despite how dark they are. A pleasant color of black. She'd think him to be a regular Swamp Hill High School student from his worn jeans and deep purple flannel.

He is quite stunning to gaze upon. But she knows he isn't worth knowing. His clear connection and surprising authority presence of Dead Fawn is enough to have her steer clear of the way his eyes consume her.

That is the type of observation she shouldn't be making right now. She's got bigger fish to fry.

"There is nothing you can do to stop the sacrifice. Everything is set in place." The man speaks in a deep voice. The sound of it rattles her bones.

July does her best not to acknowledge his words. They mean nothing to her. Not a damn thing.

She doesn't bother saying anything to him. All she does is flip him the bird and do her best to run to the truck. When she peers out of the window after quickly turning on the heating system, she finds the entire street deserted.

By the time she gets back home it's already bleeding into the afternoon and despite the cold air the sun is offering a wonderful warmth that she welcomes.

Waiting for her on the front porch is Abigail who sports the worst scowl she's ever seen from her. She must have read the note.

"See? Truck hasn't been wrecked, and I didn't use up all the gas." It's hard not to act like a smartass after escaping a crazy cult with her life somewhat intact.

Her mother shakes her head and pulls her thick sweater tighter around herself. "I was worried you might have crashed in a ditch or worse, been hijacked and held at gunpoint."

And there it is. The doubt that always seems to be present within her mother. It wouldn't be a talking-to-speech without it. So typical of her to get into trouble over nothing.

"Look, I gotta meet with the lawyer back in Dallas regarding the house. I should be back the night before you and your sister's graduation. Please, take your allergy meds and use your damn inhaler." Abigail picks up her duffle bag that July only just noticed sitting on the porch next to her mother.

She fights hard not to let her eyes roll like they normally would.

A ghastly wind blows out of the cornfield and into the trees surrounding the house. She shivers uncontrollably till it calms down again.

"Don't kill each other whenever June gets back." Abigail says as she tosses her bag into the bed of the truck.

Her heart does a flip into a gruesome pool of dread. "W-Where is she?"

Her mother shrugs before getting into the driver's seat. Of course, she fails to see that this is a huge problem.

July stumbles forth, her hands catching on the door handle, preventing her mother from shutting it.

"You have to tell me where she is." There's a good chance that it's not even her sister anymore. And that's just no good. This is so fucked.

Abigail scoffs. She's freaked by July's sudden rash behavior. Well, if she were ever around long enough, she'd have seen what the fuck has been happening in Birkstone Manor.

"I'm sure she's with her friends. Now if you'll excuse me, I got a few hours ahead of me." Her mother offers her a kind smile that is filled with false love. She knows that July is a waste of space. She could at least say something snarky like most people do.

It would lessen the blow of having always been the lesser twin.

The thought of her mother coming back home in a few days to find out only one of her daughters is alive is a damn blow to her chest. July gasps as the knowledge wounds her very spirit. She staggers backward. The back of her legs hitting the steps forcing her to collapse on them.

She may hate June with everything in her but there is a small part of her who loves her so deeply that she dreads even suggesting to herself the idea of her murder. It doesn't feel right lingering in her mind.

It's her fucking twin sister! Of course she's going to feel something like love for her. None of this is going to be easy. And yet it is for the good of the entire human race.

Yes. She should be thinking of the billions of people who for the most part are destined for some type of greatness. It's just unfortunate it has to be June to secure their lives, their souls.

Hell, thinking these only fuels her already rising guilt.

She doesn't realize she's crying until tears fall onto her bare hands that are turning pink from the chill.

This hurts. Convincing herself that this must be done hurts. It feels like someone tore open her chest and squeezed her heart till it burst in their cruel hand.

July inhales deeply. The cold air grafts to the inside of her lungs like iron. She stands tall and assesses the front lawn and the road that leads through part of the piney woods.

There might be enough time to hurriedly skim through the book and perhaps spot some alternative to murdering her own sister.

# Part III

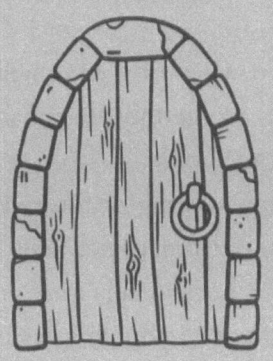

# 25. The Unknown Is Known

She's got no idea when or if June will come back to the manor tonight. So she must hurry and learn all she can from this ghastly made book.

July wastes no time running up the stairs despite the recent ache that has begun to torment her knee. With gritted teeth she hops up the steps, occasionally looking over her shoulder to make sure nothing in the house is watching her.

After everything she's witnessed so far, she wouldn't be surprised if *evil* sent something after her. Perhaps she's lucky and that He has no idea she knows the fully story.

Her chest thumps like a wild rabbit tapping its foot onto a hollowed log out in the woods.

Once inside their room she slams the door shut and takes June's vanity stool to barricade it. As she moves with the most speed and strength she can muster, she moves her dresser against the door as well. Anything heavy might buy her some time to get out of the window if something decides to attack her.

After securing the scarf she wore the other day around the doorknob to make sure it can't be pushed open, she reels back and collapses to the ground.

July flinches at the sight of more weeds and vines smothering June's side of the room. It's doing its best to take over everything. Well, that certainly is a strange way to remind her that time is running out.

The sun is setting behind her. Its vibrant yellow and orange rays shine through the window, casting all of the stained-glass colors around her as she clutches the book for dear life.

She takes a few deep breaths, willing her heart to calm before she ends up having a panic attack. Actually, it may be an asthma attack. Now as she dwells on it, she has no idea where her inhaler is.

Oops. There's no time to go out on the hunt for it.

July doesn't bother flipping on the light switch. It's long since been buried underneath the vines that sprout oddly pale green leaves that smell like spoiled meat. It's proving difficult to cope with the scents.

She shakes her head. Forcing herself to pay attention to hidden keys that may lie inked in these pages.

She scoots across the floor and takes out her small flashlight. It's enough light to make the damned book readable.

Her heavy sigh ruffles the first few pages. The movement of the rustic paper fills her nose with a pleasant smell that reminds her of the school library.

That comparison brings her a touch of momentary comfort. It soon comes to an end as she takes a shaky finger to flip to the next page. The small smile she once had melts into a depressing frown.

*Keep doing that and you'll get wrinkles. No need to make you uglier than you already are.*

June's sickly-sweet voice enters her mind, obstructing her concentration abruptly. She shakes her head to clear it away.

July leans closer to the book and lets her eyes soak in everything that if offers her. She's got no choice. This is the worst reading assignment of her life.

These few pages are the small history of Swamp Hill. It only makes her wonder who they plan to use for the sacrifice. There haven't been any missing persons posters displayed anywhere. The cult of Dead Fawn will certainly stop her if she attempts anything. But does she have the guts to kill her own sister? She likes to think that there must be some other way to end June's suffering. Maybe the librarian she's grown to admire missed something. Yes. That's one way to think positively.

It gives a brief overview of what Dead Fawn suspected *evil* of doing when He was free. Such as influencing the worst of plagues and unexplainable natural disasters that never would have happened on their own.

They want not only His approval but some of His power to ruin those who oppose their ways. How pathetic does that sound? Really fucking pathetic.

Her eyes drift upward in less than a second it seems. A warm draft has filled the room which is certainly fucking strange because it was pretty much freezing earlier. And yet she feels drops of sweat sliding down her face and into the neck of her sweater.

"Fuck. You." She mutters in a whisper. Hoping that *evil* can hear her and feel every ounce of disrespect she tries to gather.

It's answered with an increase in this sudden heatwave. Almost like someone's hot breath hits the back of her neck, wrapping around her heated skin.

July reaches behind her to swat it away. It does no good. She's practically dying in this unwanted warmth.

Ignoring all these attempts to dissuade her from the task of saving her sister's soul, July turns a few more pages to digest anything else that may prove useful.

According to this book, the white deer appears with tears in its eyes to someone of a troubled soul that may have enough internal strength to stop the ritual. It will continue to weep, giving a warning that it will only get worse.

Jeez, as if she hadn't already noticed that shit was getting a little insane.

With a roll of her eyes, she skips this page and lands on the one about all those damn irritating butterflies. She found a few of them two nights ago lingering in the hallways and bathroom. And yet none of them approached the room where June sleeps. They're funny little bugs.

Their presence is meant to further warn the one the white deer searched for and chose to end this quest to release *evil* from His eternal prison. They are beacons to show the way of the darkness His power conjures or whatever this book is trying to say. The words start to get muddy and don't make a lick of sense anymore.

Something about the deer's chosen that they must stop at nothing to keep Dead Fawn from opening the door. Well, that's what she plans to do anyway.

She scoffs and rolls back on her ankles. July rubs her face, whipping sweat off her temple. It's so hot and now she can hear the vines and weeds and flowers growing. They produce a sickening scratching noise that makes her squeamish.

She goes over the previous pages a second time. It's hopeless to wish for anything helpful. But it's all warnings that she has already known. That doesn't require a genius, fortunately.

After discovering nothing useful she moves on and winds through to the middle of the book.

There she finds a page talking about the blue moon and its purpose.

"Now we're talkin'." July allows a grin to spread on her lips.

Her pointer finger trembles as she carefully glides it over the paper that feels incredibly fragile.

This is pretty straight forward. The blue moon generates enough power to heighten preexisting magic when it's needed. And of course, *evil* discovered this all those years ago and He must have possessed someone. It gives Him almost infinite power. But each time Dead Fawn attempted the ritual someone foiled their plans.

The book says it was always a family member or close friend that the deer appeared before, marking them as the chosen one. No wonder the Birkstone family died in mysterious ways before the even reached their fifties. They were close to someone chosen to make the sacrifice, forcing them to step in and stop it.

It sounds like an awful job to have. And she's so damn unlucky to be one of them. It's completely unfair. But it makes sense.

The *evil* chose June to perform the sacrifice and give her body over to Him once He gets out. The white deer chose July to put an end to it. Still so different from each other. Being a twin sucks ass.

July brings her light closer to the book in hopes of somehow reading through the crossed-out section of this passage. It's hard to read through the red stuff that marks it out. Her eyes go wide. July drops the book in a hurry.

Someone went through this book and ruined certain information on purpose by using blood. She has no doubt that it's human.

There is no way to determine what it says. She's out of luck with that one.

July breaks out into a large yawn. Her jaw pops and her eyelids threaten to droop shut.

Damn, she's been crisscrossed on the floor for hours. It's late and she hasn't heard June come into the house. Actually, she may not have heard if she did. June hasn't been herself in weeks and has done unexplainable things. She could be more silent than a field mouse if she wanted. If *evil* wanted her to be.

She sets the book onto her night table after getting off the floor. Her bones pop and squeal.

Mental exhaustion surely weights a person down. July feels it fester in her being. Sleep is calling out to her, and she doesn't have the energy to change into pajamas. Her eyes clamp shut the second she plops on her bed and lets her head hit the pillow. The fear of June possibly getting inside the room doesn't compare to her will to sleep.

July is out like a candle flame being blown to silence, forbidden to flicker until it's lit once more.

# 26. June The Possessed

Dreams… well… more like nightmares plagued her deep sleep. She couldn't escape the guilt that her subconscious pushed into her mind. All of it consumed even the possibility of a pleasant dream. There was no place she could run to.

Her mind birthed images of June slaughtering everyone in the school. Students and teachers screamed in fear. The sounds made her heart quake with unease and devastation. People trampled over others trying to get away from the girl dressed in her cheer uniform covered in their blood and chilling yellow eyes that glowed bright.

July stood at the opposite end of the turmoil with a strange wood stake in her heads. She remembered looking upon the weapon with a deer branded into the wood. It was a taunting joke.

Cruel in its urging for her to stop the ritual and keep *evil* in His prison.

All but telling her to murder her sister for the greater good.

She'd be lying if she admitted even to herself that she's more than prepared to do it.

July gasps with a troubling start the moment June stops her wicked crusade of death and destruction in front of her in the blood-bathed hallways.

Her body wakes her before June can rip her throat out with the bizarre needle-like teeth that have taken over her mouth.

As she sits on the edge of her bed watching the afternoon sun slowly sink behind the cornfield and piney woods July knows He wanted her to see that.

This damn *evil* got in her head. Violating her dreams. Forcing them into whatever He wanted her to witness.

It's the vilest experience she'd ever been a witness too. Yet as she gets up off the bed to change into a new sweater made from soft ivory material to get out of the one smelling of old sweat, July knows it's what the future will bring. It's disappointing how obvious that is.

Saying that there is a damn good chance she won't lift a finger in her sister's direction.

It doesn't lessen the sting of knowing His intentions of June. More than she wants it to, it hurts to have this knowledge and no one to share it with. She's alone in this. Perhaps that's the point of it all.

She alone is meant to somehow stop her possessed sister from being a murderer.

No pressure. Not like the fate of Swamp Hill and the rest of the world is in her hands.

Oh, shit. That's what it feels like. So much is weighing on her shoulders. She didn't want any of this shit either.

July gathers her hair in a tight ponytail towards the crown of her head. Her thick bangs drape over her glasses. She must look like a joke dressed in dirty jeans and this sweater. Good thing she isn't trying to get on *evil's* good graces and impress Him.

In fact, looking and acting ordinary is what almost everyone expects of her. If she keeps up this ridiculous charade, then they won't see her final move coming.

She glances around the room while it's still filled with the outside light. She slept the entire day. The sun is just starting to set. Time is running out.

All the plant growth on June's side has finally managed to start slithering its way over to July's. A few stray vines flicker at her feet as she moves towards the door. She can't pinpoint the source of the soft squeaks that flutter into the room. The noise causes chills to rush down her spine.

Her body does an unexpected quiver.

Almost like it intends to stop her. Another person or thing being influenced by the darkness trapped on the other side of the purple door.

She finds an old wood baseball bat hidden beneath the kitchen sink after scouring the entire house for any potential weapons to protect herself against June.

Her lips tug into a wide grin. Relief floods her chest as her hands wrap around the worn handle, daggering her fingers into the leather binding.

This is better than her idea to risk leaving the manor to search in the tool shed.

A big ass stick like this may be easier to wield instead of one of those knives that Abigail stashes in a large cookie jar near the fridge. She thinks that July has no idea that they're hidden there. Well, July needed to map out possible things she could use to defend herself if she was able to get access to them and she found them after her exploration.

And yet this heavy baseball bat seems more fitting for her habit of being clumsy. Wherever she swings it's bound to hit something.

July scoots back out from under the sink. She wobbles onto her feet. Her knee threatens to dislocate but she makes sure to position her foot to keep it in place.

All the confidence she did muster as she trudged down the stairs earlier drains out of her as she catches a glimpse of June standing in the back door's frame.

She gulps and tucks the bat behind her, hoping that June fails to notice.

"You don't look so good, June." Her words tremble from either sudden adrenaline or fear. It's too soon to tell the difference.

Her sister is a walking corpse. There isn't hardly any muscles on her bones. Whatever she had for cheer and all the other activities she once took part in is completely gone. Those bones of hers stick out from beneath her ruined cheer uniform. It's covered in dirt and something that oddly resembles blood. How comforting.

June tilts her head to the side. The movement is harsh and clearly uncoordinated as she almost topples over due to her head going lopsided in such a quick manner.

And yet she can't help but feel sorry for June. Her eyes are completely sunken in. The part of her skull is so prominent that her eye sockets act like caves that are filled with glowing yellow light. Beacons in a dark storm that trick people into false safety.

July isn't going to fall for it. Not again. Not ever fucking again.

She slowly squares her shoulders as June begins to roam her inhuman eyes over her body, latching onto something that she isn't. June won't ever be whole again; she's far too gone.

She can see that now. Her sister died the night she failed to reach her before she made her way to the door. It's too late to wish for her to take it back now. What's done is done.

July inhales a shaky breath. Tears prick at her eyes. An emotional pain strikes inside of her chest. That thing behind the door, it's ruined June to where July can't remember what she's supposed to look like.

Her sister's lips are blackened and cracked beyond salvation. The corners of her mouth have been spilt, allowing her smile to be more sinister and disturbing. Fuck. Why is she smiling at her like that?

Almost every exposed inch of her pale gray skin is covered in old wounds and fresh cuts that leak an awful color that resemble rotten corn. June's blood has long since turned a gross purple shade that covers her as well. It's a great contrast to the yellow snot that keeps leaking from her nose and mouth.

Every ounce of teenage girl she once has been eaten away. Devoured.

No matter how much hate she had in her heart for June, she never wanted this for her. It's such a pity. That sparks anger in her. July grips the bat tighter, standing as still as she can when June takes three steps forth.

"You don't look much better, Sparky." Her sister's voice is rough and has a rasp to it that fails to bring comfort.

She'll miss her high-pitched squeals and snorting laughter.

July's mouth curls upward. "At least I'm better off than you."

The possessed June chuckles darkly. The sound echoes into the kitchen. It encourages a troubling feeling to rumble in her guts. That's a noise she doesn't want to think about too hard.

In a sudden burst, June cackles louder. A chain reaction occurs as a clash of thunder and a strike of lightening follow it after.

The bright blue streak that sputters in the sky illuminates the inside of the kitchen just as the lights blow out. Every light bulb in the vicinity bursts, the glass clattering to the tiled floor.

She jolts, momentarily glancing over her shoulder. July's dull brown eyes go wide at the sight of multiple members of Dead Fawn slipping out from behind furniture and other things, revealing their summoned presence.

Shit. How long have they been in the manor?

When she staggers back around, she shouts in surprise. June is less than a foot away from her. A waft of intense rotting breath seeps into her nostrils. She fails to contain her gag.

The noise only entices June. Her sister grins wickedly and leans close to sniff her, inhaling whatever the fuck she's smelling.

July's hands are starting to sweat. She struggles to keep a firm hold on the bat. Her fingers bite into the worn leather wrapping so harshly that splinters quickly embed into her. With all her will she doesn't shout or groan in pain.

Some have said it hasn't rained in Swamp Hill for a year. Others say for much longer. And yet it matters not as she hears rain pelt against the manor, sliding down the multicolored glass.

This time she's more than certain that it's real. Not like the times *evil* was playing tricks on her to weaken the ragged spirit in her.

"You are lucky that He hasn't chosen you to be sliced in two for the sacrifice. Instead, *evil* has ordered you to watch. Isn't that exciting? I sure think it is." June coughs a little, yellow spit landing on July's face.

It's cold tone. There is no ounce of warmth inside of June. Maybe her being dead isn't such a far reach after all.

June makes a clicking sound with her mouth that's followed by another flash of lightning.

She hears rapid heavy footsteps. They're coming for her on June's order. Fuck that.

July ducks down and wails aloud as her knees pop harshly in protest. However, it doesn't stop her from hurrying on her knees to get away from June and the Dead Fawn goons.

Heavy breathing fills her ears as June attempts to grab her. July shouts as she aims a kick at her sister's boney leg.

Once she hears a sickening crack it's enough to fuel her movements. She uses one side of the kitchen island to hoist herself up.

On the opposite side is June with His followers. They all sport the same expression. Anger tinged with fear. Hmm. Of course, they're afraid of *evil* despite what He must have promised them all.

That doesn't surprise her in the least. She's starting to think that this fucker can't do anything himself. He's got an entire cult of followers and is forced to corrupt a teenage girl for His own gain. Now that's beyond pathetic. It's almost laughable.

"You can't escape this, July. He, the one who promises the most beautiful riches, wants you to join us. Now, stop acting like a little bitch and accept this rare and truly generous invitation." As she says each word every male Dead Fawn follower gradually creeps around the island, trapping July with no room for escape.

Despite the fear that begs her to succumb to this, to let it play out and hope that they won't kill her right after, July clenches her jaws.

"I know June isn't in there. Not anymore. But I do know it's you, *evil*. Hear this. Fuck. You." The words are intoxicating venom on her tongue. It's liberating.

June screeches madly. The sound vibrates her bones. Shaking the entire manor like an earthquake.

The older guy to July's right with unruly black hair and alarmingly bright green eyes stutters forward with out-stretched hands ready to get a hold of her.

"Shit!" July decides now is the best time to use the bat.

She swings it with a grunt. It lands on his shoulder. An audible snap fills her ears. He falls back with a strangled cry clutching his most likely shattered shoulder. Hell yeah.

Her slight victory is short lived once a large hand digs into her back. She twists around and fails to hit the other guy with pale skin and dirt colored hair. He kicks her ankle with his large brown boots mainly used when rounding up cattle.

July collapses against the edge of the nearest counter. Her arms flail across the counter surface, failing to find purchase. She momentarily pauses as her eyes manage to find the cookie jar and the guy takes a hold of her hips.

She's so close to getting it open after lunging in his grip to grab it. July rips it back. However, as the guy does his best to pin her arms she's forced to drop the jar, letting it fall and break into a hundred pieces along with the knives.

It matters not. June has grown impatient. She can tell by the way her eyes squint at her.

The guy keeping her still then pushes her forward, sending her over the island and right into June's open arms.

Her shocked shout ends the second June slaps her across the face. The sting of the hit puts her in overdrive. July scurries across the floor avoiding the other's legs like obstacles in a summer camp course.

She manages to get close to the recently discarded knives. Her fingers just barely graze the handle of one. July cries as she's roughly flipped on her back. All the breath in her lungs fleeing at once. June climbs on top of her and gets her hands on her throat.

Black pricks at her vision. She fails to inhale any air. June's suffocating her.

July's silent begging to die quickly is answered in the opposite way she's asking.

Her sister releases her, enjoying the way her choking gasps consume the atmosphere.

After a few more smacks to the face and punches to her chest June yanks her up by the collar of her shirt. She groans in protests. No amount of scratching and leg kicking causes her to let her go.

Those who tried their best to detain her come around. One binds her hands with an old worn rope. Another covers her head with a burlap sack that sticks to the new tears that leak down her face.

June tosses her into someone's arms. They lead her kicking and screaming out of Birkstone Manor. They live far enough outside of town that no one can hear her.

Her feet drag along the marble steps. She fails to find purchase on anything. There's no way she can grip the columns to yank herself free.

Despite the sack round her head, she can still smell the moist air. The ground is certainly squishy from the rain that continues to pound over them. It sinks into her sweater, causing her undershirt and bra to meld into one solid piece.

Her shoes are dragging through the mud. Some of it flicks onto her pants, soaking her knees and thighs in an instant.

They ignore her protests to ease up their grips. Instead, they slam her to the ground, her knees quickly sinking into the soft ground.

A moment later someone comes over to rip the sack off her head.

It takes a little bit for her eyes to adjust. The second she does, July realizes they shattered her glasses during their brawl. Pieces are missing from the lenses. Fucking bastards.

The moon that's swelling with an unnatural blue glow shine above them all. There's at least twenty people here. All of them circling the purple door that's adorned with strands of those awful vines and many candles that haven't been put out by the rain. They really have been waiting a long time for this.

With her hands bound behind her back there's no way she can get away now.

"The moon is getting close to its highest peak. Let's begin." June croaks. Her voice continues to get more disastrous and nastier. Spit flies from her mouth, infiltrating the seemingly pure rain drops the town hasn't seen in a long time.

It's a shame that something along the lines of a small miracle is tainted by utter evil.

July watches her move behind another figure on their knees. She fails to recognize the person on the account of not being able to make out their clothes from over here.

But as June tears the burlap sack off the other captive's head, she feels the blood drain from her face. Her chest stutters. The blood pumping organ keeping her alive skips exactly three beats.

The sight of the beaten Ms. Tibbs, the intended sacrifice, has July break out into a hoarse sob.

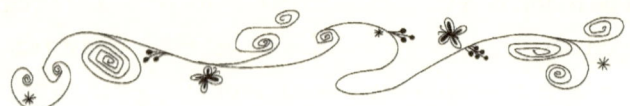

# 27. Blue Moon

Her sobs, filled with burning turmoil, melt into pained shouts. The heartbreaking sounds ruffle the hundreds of monarch butterflies that have somehow been blessed not to get wet in the rain. They've been lingering in the cornstalks and trees that line the field leading to the swamps.

They swarm the purple door and Dead Fawn members, attacking in their strange ways.

A few of them land gracefully onto her shoulders. They fail to give her comfort. Nothing will ever ease the pain that swells inside her body and soul.

July gathers her sobs, stuffing them back down into her being. Her chest heaves with each hiccup that ravages her.

The sorrow that's gradually consuming her only grows fiercer when she catches sight of that damn white deer slowly walking out of the stalks.

It gazes at her with its massive eyes that never fail to produce a tear. But its horrible shriek of despair rocks her deeply. The sound is blood-chilling. And yet she knows it's meant to strike a feeling within her. She manages to understand what it wanted to tell her all those weeks ago.

July needs to get up and fight. To do something before it really is too fucking late and *evil* is free.

*Yeah. I'm right on it. No need to feel any more fear. Your fucking chosen one is on the case!*

Even her inner thoughts are laced with sarcasm. Well, anything is better than self-hatred.

The deer gives another scream. This time the noise guides July back to her feet as if an invisible hand has grabbed hold of her shirt, hoisting her quickly upward. She stumbles slightly within the ever-growing wave of butterflies. They continue attacking the followers and June despite the heavy downpour.

"Stop fucking around. They're just pathetic ugly bugs!" June's anger can be seen and felt. Her thin brows furrow as she gets behind Ms. Tibbs and whacks her on the back of the head. The older woman gives a pained yelp.

July frowns deeply. Her feet beg for her to move ahead and somehow stop June.

It's the sudden voices in her head that stop her from doing a damn thing. Her sister hears them too. They are the only ones who do. The others don't stop at all.

In unison, the sisters look upon the purple door. The wood looks like it's glowing from the moon and quivering from the power it's keeping trapped.

Oh, Fuck.

*"I can grant all your wishes. Give you the power to end those who make a fool of you. Doesn't that sound lovely? Enticing? Please, aid your sister in freeing me from this excruciating prison."* That's the voice that's done its best to haunt her nightmares. The *evil* is more awake than ever.

He must be saying something different to June. She smiles madly and nods her head in a quick rhythm. Whatever His words are, it must be extremely satisfying. She watches her sister drop to her knees and sets her hands in a praying position. She looks terrible.

July shakes her head. "No thanks." She says aloud.

The door gives a groaning rumble. The *evil* on the other side wails. It's a ghastly sound. Almost like a goat. The thought of that has her curling in on herself, tucking her head to her shoulder.

*"Then you shall be the first of my hundreds of well-deserving victims. I shall bathe in your coward blood, let it seep into my body, the one I'll rightfully take from your pathetic sister. You cannot hide from me, July. I see right through you."* He sneers into her mind.

The force of it has her knees trembling.

"You're insane." She croaks into the open. June whips her head around in an instant.

"You don't get to decide who or what I am, you fucking cocksucker." July spits with more anger than she intended. Yet it gets the point across especially with language like that. She's not going to lie about it having felt so good to say.

It roars in her head as well as June's. The corrupted twin stumbles backward. Her face scrunches in confusion and fear.

For a moment, July is tempted to go comfort her. But it's her sister's brightly glowing yellow eyes that suggest otherwise.

She flinches as June gets up in a flash.

"Why the hell are y'all fucking around for? We've got a ritual to perform!" Her order carries out sharply.

July inhales a shallow breath before gripping the rope tied around her hands and makes a run for it. Directly into the piney woods and swamps that bleed into it.

Despite June's aggravated shouts and pleas of displeasure, July keeps going no matter that she doesn't have a clue where she's headed.

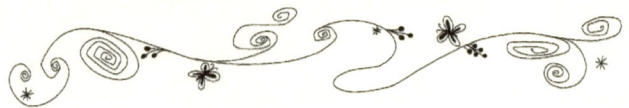

# 28. Chase Me, Sis

Her legs move the best they can despite the permanent limp her bad knee has caused. The feel of June's burning gaze on her back fuels her might, aiding her momentum to keep going.

She must lead June away from the purple door for as long as she can. July has to do everything to make sure her sister isn't there when the blue moon meets its highest peak.

Then all of this stupid shit will be for nothing.

It was a miracle that she didn't make the rash decision to escape through the cornstalks. That would have been the worst. She's sure June knows her way in and out of that maze like the back of her hand. July would've been a goner if that happened.

Her lungs contract. There's an ache in her chest from breathing roughly. But at least she isn't freezing.

The rain that seeps through the thick tree canopy onto her shoulders is rather warm. A rise in temperature has somehow kept her from becoming an icicle like most nights.

"C'mon, July. I can fucking smell your fear. You're such a little pussy. No wonder Daddy didn't want us!" June screeches from somewhere behind her.

It's unfortunate that the words pack a punch. They stab her heart, digging into her being like a sickening burn. June always knew exactly what to say to hurt her.

It shouldn't matter. June isn't in there anymore. It's mere fuel that she consumes. This thing, *evil*, is using her to get what He wants. She won't let it.

She keeps her mouth shut and weaves through the thick trees that smell of moist moss and the slight speckle of sourness. The ground sinks under her feet. Sometimes attempting to sink her in.

The moon is so bright that July is able to make out the most basic of shapes like the trees, boulders, and the stream that leads to the swamp that's inhabited by all kinds of creatures. The animal she rather not see again is that alligator. She had enough of it the last time the beast ate her leg!

A snap echoes behind her. July swerves to the left. Her foot slips. She collapses against a tall droopy willow tree that has long been hollowed.

With surprisingly little effort July manages to climb into the hole in the tree. It's big enough to engulf her entirely.

Well, it seems that being small and fragile does have some perks.

*Take that, June!*

It's a pity she's too frightened and pissed to shout out loud. She needs a moment to figure out what her next move is.

*Crunnnch! Crrunchhhh! Ssnahp!*

Footsteps make their way over to her. She bites the inside of her cheek so hard that she can now taste her own blood. Ugh, this iron taste makes her stomach gurgle.

July swallows the blood and a scream as she hears June get closer.

She pushes further into the hole. Her back hits the very far wall. Her eyes go wide as something in the waistline of her pants cuts her skin.

Realization swells within her. In a hurry, she retrieves it and quickly cuts her hands free. Though she doesn't get off that easily. She does more than give herself paper cuts along her fingers and wrists. July inwardly groans from the new sting.

With the newly bloodied kitchen knife the size of her forearm in hand, July holds it to her chest and listens.

She keeps her breathing deep despite the way her lungs scream at her not to. It's the only way she can calm her racing heart. And besides, June can certainly hear her frantic huffs a mile away with the rain suddenly letting up again. Shit.

"July! Come out, please. I didn't mean what I said before." Her giggles give away her true thoughts on the matter. "It can't be helped that you're a pathetic weasel that can never stand up for herself. Honestly, everyone knows you're going to die a virgin. As if a guy would ever slip his dick in you. Let me do you a favor and chop off your toes and feed them to you!" June sounds worse than she did before.

Her words are croaky. July can hear the scratching of her throat. It is almost as if someone is choking her. Another way she knows it's *evil* contorting her for His bidding.

July takes another moment to let her sister move around the area to scout for her. After hearing her stumbling steps travel further away she uses this moment to search the hole she's occupying.

Her fingers grasp onto a broke log. It's small enough that she can use one hand to hold it. A good chance to use it for her advantage.

She forms a crazy plan. It might prove to be a decent distraction. But if it fails then she might as well kiss her boring allergy-filled life goodbye.

June continues to move further ahead. July leans out of the hole, her legs spilling over the jagged edge. She buries the wail of pain she desperately wants to let out as the tree digs into her pants and tears her flesh.

More blood drips down the back of her thighs and knees. Ignoring this new unwanted warmth, July raises her hand containing the piece of log and chunks it rather close to her right.

Her sister's movements stop for a moment before they start back again and this time in her direction.

"Shit." July mumbles and moves to hide behind the willow. She clutches its trunk for dear life.

She only needs June to get close enough for her plan to work. Too close and those sharp teeth of hers will surely rip out her throat.

"Damn, I can smell your soul. It will please Him greatly to feast upon it. Why don't you come out and- "June isn't able to finish her sentence as July hurries to bombard her space with wide raging brown eyes and the kitchen knife held high next to her head.

Her sister doesn't get the chance to fight back. The knife is sticking out her chest. The fresh wound is leaking blood that's blackened and smells like rot. The yellow in her eyes starts to flicker like the flash of a lightening bug.

With an unexpected gag July steps backward. She moves to clamp her nostrils shut. Her foot catches on an exposed tree root and it sends her to the ground, smearing mud all over her.

Her sister stares at her intently before raising her hand to somehow remove the knife.

"No!" July stumbles to her feet and rushes to grip June in a staggering embrace. She takes the hilt and gives it a firm twist. Her sister groans with pain. Good. She and the *evil* deserve it.

A new angle of blue moonlight cascades upon them. It's at its highest peak. June didn't perform the sacrifice. July stopped Him from getting out. But is the cost truly worth it?

She feels the ground beneath her feet tremble. He is angry. He should be. No way was she going to let Him out.

June's black blood has an odd yellow shimmering sheen to it. It glows in the moonlight. It's dripping in a rushing river from her chest, eyes, and mouth. Probably her ears too. She doesn't want to look to confirm that.

June leans over to the side forcing July down with her. She gets on her knees to cradle her. It's an awful position. A truly gut-wrenching way to look upon one's dying sister. And of course that's happening. June's body is dying.

She knows her sister isn't in there anymore but that doesn't make this hurt any less.

Her bottom lip quivers. Tears fall from her eyes onto June's pale flesh. She never wanted this. July doesn't want her sister to die despite how naturally evil she is. It isn't supposed to be this way.

"I hate you for doing this to me, June." Her mumbled words shake.

July uses a bruised hand to gently caress her sister's brow. Oh, she'd be so pissed if she knew they hadn't been done in weeks. Perhaps this is a small blessing.

She sniffs, letting snot trail down the back of her throat. "You put this on me. I had no fucking choice. Can't you see that? You did this to us."

There really is no point in talking. June can't hear her. Not from where she's at. No genius is required to know where *evil* has sent her soul.

"I should be glad that I stopped *evil* from getting out. But I'm not. I'm angry that you couldn't fight His wishes and pleas. That His words were too enticing even for the fucking independent June to ignore. I'm ashamed that I couldn't save you. God, that's so fucked up, isn't it?" Her cries only deepen in sound.

Her chest quakes. There's a pounding in her skull. She feels a sneeze build in the far reaches of her sinuses.

She begins to caress June's wispy blonde hair that has long lost its shine.

"You might have been b-born an evil bitch, but you're m-my sister." Sobs engulf her body.

July leans over her, clutching June to her chest. She does not hide her wails. Instead, she lets them free. Her cries wrap around the trees. Birds nestled in their branches flutter their wings and take flight. Crickets chirp and grasshoppers flutter their legs. She can hear gators slide back into the nearby stream, heading back to their dens in the swamp.

So much life surrounds this place and yet the one person she never had the chance to truly love is gone.

Her heart crumbles as she watches with blurry vision the yellow haze in June's eyes fade into nothingness. The body of June Birkstone is gone. Her soul is in an entirely different plain than this.

July's mouth wobbles. She can't contain the tortured shout that she produces. Her bones tingle with the sound. Her fingers grip the dead body, leaving imprints in the soiled skin and ruined muscles.

An unnatural cloud of hazy purple tinged with dots of yellow seeps out of June's mouth. She guesses that *evil's* grasp on her sister is truly no more.

She did it at a cost that she never expected.

Her cruel sister.

Her nasty other half.

Her *twin.*

# Part IV

# 29. Midnight

The muscles in her legs scream at her with each step forth she takes. The rain might have stopped for a while but that doesn't mean the ground will dry up in an instant.

There's a slight pain in her left wrist that hadn't been too torn up by the knife still embedded in the body's chest. July continues to drag it behind her. An ache threatens to overwhelm her back. However, she can't stop yet.

After a while the blue moon shifts in the sky. It's reached midnight. There will be no sacrifice tonight.

That knowledge encourages a smile to embrace her lips. She lets it spread across her face as she breaks through the tree line and back into the cornfield.

Her eyes grow wide at the sight of the many stalks quickly deteriorating. Their rotting stench surging into her nose. She gulps down a gag.

The few Dead Fawn members square up as she makes her way with the heavy body to the purple door.

She can feel *evil's* shouts do their best to penetrate her mind. July enforces her mental walls with imaginary iron bars. Keeping Him out isn't so hard now that his main source of power is no more.

It's sadder to know that the Devil himself is the likely culprit that put *evil* in His prison.

July sniffs harshly and ignores the snot that trails down her lips and chin. She gives a grunt and shrugs the limp body before them. Most gasp. Others growl in frustration. It must suck to fail once again to please their master. Good thing she doesn't give two shits about their feelings.

An older boy who has long black hair and black eyes steps forward with a whimpering Ms. Tibbs in hand. Her eyes widen slightly with realization. It's the same guy who warned her in town yesterday.

He's got a knife in his large veiny hand, holding it up to her tan throat.

Tears slip down her flushed cheeks. She can see the front of her pants dampen. Poor woman pisses herself out of fear.

She makes the decision not to look in her direction any longer.

"You won't be unlocking that door. At least not with me still breathing. Unfortunately for you I plan to live for a very long time." She says despite the crack in her tone.

The black-haired boy shrugs, allowing the knife to further nip Ms. Tibbs. The woman groans in pain. A trickle of fresh blood leaks down her neck.

"Alright. It looks like we ain't gonna have ourselves a party after all." He tells the others. They begin to move around and pack up all the materials and tools intended for the ritual.

July nudges her chin outward and hopes he'll take it as a sign of resistance.

The corner of his lips quirk, revealing his surprisingly white teeth.

"I don't wanna to catch Dead Fawn on Birkstone property ever again. You think y-y'all can manage that?" She shrugs her shoulders as well. Too can play at this.

"I promise you nothing, July Birkstone. When another blue moon presents itself there is no stopping Him." He tells her while keeping a firm grip on the librarian.

"Please." Ms. Tibbs cries out to her. She ignores it.

"I'll be ready if the time comes." She nods her head firmly. A deal has struck between her and the cult. She hopes they won't try anything. There is nothing for her to live for anymore besides keeping the door closed.

He says nothing more but returns her nod. Then the blade against the woman's throat moves in a quick motion. Gurgling erupts into the late-night air. The stench of fresh blood consumes them.

Gah, she's had enough of that smell. It carries in the wind, slipping into her nose without invitation.

July makes no move to comfort her or attempt to stop the bleeding. Even if she managed to reach her, nothing can be done to save her.

Her heart clenches again only this time in pity. The woman might have been her friend, but friends get in the way in the end of all things dangerous and evil. She should have known better than to help a cursed family such as the Birkstones.

She doesn't shed any tears for the woman. The boy wipes his bloody hands onto his black button up shirt and gives her a devilish wink. July swallows her disgust.

July watches him click his tongue at a younger boy. He in return takes the freshly dead woman and drags her along with them. That leaves her with June's body to take care of.

What a bunch of little fuckers.

# 30. Eternal Slumber

Dragging the empty body proves to be more difficult this time.

July is worn out and completely drained. Why couldn't Dead Fawn take this one with them? After all, it had been their fucking responsibility since day one. Leave it to women to take care of a man's problem. Such pathetic assholes.

She has no doubt that the older boy with long black hair is the cult leader. It's a good guess that the position is handed down on the account of the cult being so old.

She hopes it'll be quite some time before they cross paths again.

It won't be the worst idea to further research them and prepare for more of their frail attempts at releasing the evil.

The girl has been tugging the dead body of her sister to the far back of the cornfield. The only place she is certain people won't look for June. Plus, that's where the tool shed resides. There's a good chance she'll find a shovel in there to dig a hole eight feet deep.

She isn't going to risk any search dogs catching her scent through the soil if the police look for her.

July lugs the body to an abrupt stop. It lands on the ground with a thud. Various birds and small animals give a slight shout before hurrying away. They too feel the echo of *evil* and His darkness.

With a rather pointy rock, July manages to break the lock on the shed door. After opening it, letting the door swing against the outside of the shed, a gust of old dust wafts into her face. She unwillingly inhales the particles and gives a rough sneeze. That has been lingering within her for a while now. Good thing she can get past it to search for a shovel.

She digs through the various piles of rope and scans the hooks holding several different types of tools. By pure luck does she find a flashlight sitting on a small table right next to the door. July sighs in relief to find that the batteries in it still work.

The light drifts around the shed. This place is filled with all kinds of junk. But once her eyes catch sight of a chipped shovel at the very back her frown quickly morphs into a triumphant smile.

July hurries to retrieve it. Dried blood crumbles over her body as she moves to get it in her ruined hands.

She doesn't dare hiss in pain as the handle of the shovel makes contact with her sliced palms. There are more important things to worry about than her newly reopened wounds leaking fresh blood.

The girl wipes the blood on her pants before she makes it out of the shed.

There's a chill in the air now. Must be getting closer to the early morning hours. She can't waste any more time fooling around.

July has the shovel in one hand and takes June's limp wrist in the other. With a grand heave she moves ahead to search for the best spot.

A grin curls on her lips as she finds a nice plump willow at the very edge of the tree line. This is the perfect place to let her sister rest. She's sure June would somehow find it in her evil heart to thank her for this.

She lets her sister's body hit the ground for another time and stabs the point of the shovel right into the ground.

The muscles in her shoulders and back of her thighs burn, screaming at July to stop this ridiculous funeral that means absolutely nothing.

Sweat trails down the sides of her face. A few drops sink into her eyes. The sting of it causes her to cry out and toss away her shattered glasses.

"Fuck." A hiss flees through her cracked lips.

Once she regains a slightly better vision- still it's a mess- July gives a troubled sigh and looks at the body.

"You know, I always though you looked stupid in those hair curlers. I was too afraid to say something. You have a habit of hitting me when I say things you don't particularly like." She doesn't allow a sickening smile to grace her lips.

Had. Her sister *had* a habit of doing mean and sadistic things to her. That's never going to happen again. She won't miss it either.

She gives a limp cackle and continues to toss dirt out of the ever-growing hole in the ground. The generous rain has made it much easier to sink the shovel into and rip the soil out.

Snot drips down her nose. She pauses for a moment to wipe it off with her torn sleeve. July does nothing to stop her tears.

"You were evil way before He decided that you were His to take. But I should have known something was wrong. It was right in front of my face. And yet I still had no clue. If only you were still in there to warn me. But you must have given up with ease, you fucker." July curses a few more times as she hurriedly throws dirt out of the hole.

She can't decide what's worse. Her sister's body is void of any soul and breath or her anger towards someone who isn't alive to hear her angered words. Now who's the pathetic one? Oh yeah, it's fucking July Birkstone.

July rolls her shoulders and makes the decision to take off her sweater and finish the job in just her jeans and bra. Any second longer beneath all that material and she'll die over from heat stroke.

"You ruined my life the moment we were born different. And this is just the cherry on top of the fucked-up cake." She growls as she accidentally hits a tree root.

In quick spurts she jabs the tip of the shovel into it and breaks it apart. July gets down on her knees and yanks the broken root out with her bare hands. She turns around slightly to toss it away.

Having used such a strike of energy has her panting. She looks over to the body and spits at it in aggravation. Yeah. That'll show June. She suddenly wishes June can see from the other side or at least hear her from wherever He took her soul to.

Bright blue moon light moves from out behind a few dark gray rain clouds. Its beautiful rays shine down upon her. Why does something so pretty have to be used for something so foul? She guesses there is no real answer to that.

July twirls her dirty hands, gripping her fingers to expel the nerves swelling within her. "Despite everything I still love you, June. You might have hated me most of the time, but I know you loved me too in your strange way. Like when you wouldn't let someone else bully me without your permission. I was always grateful that you took account of who did what to me. It's okay."

With another sniffle she determines that the hole is deep enough.

She crawls on her throbbing knees to the body. As she takes in the sight of June's rapidly decaying flesh her brows furrow. It won't be the worst idea to at least shroud her in something.

Even the previously possessed deserve a proper burial.

That includes June Birkstone.

July slowly gets back on her aching feet to return to the tool shed and find something useful.

She comes back with an old worn blue tarp. There's no telling what it was once used for but now it will be the blanket to keep June's body warm while it rots. Damn. That thought gives her stomach a squeeze. Perhaps that's hunger talking.

It takes a few minutes to flatten out the tarp and roll the body into it. And then another set of minutes to wrap it around the body, tucking in the excess flaps to keep it from sliding out.

Her own limbs are tired. It's best to get on with this. She will still require time to mourn. Someone must.

July takes a deep breath that rattles her lungs. Her fingers grip one side of the body. With a huff she pushes it over the edge and right into the newly dug hole.

It's much easier to put the dirt back in.

The shovel moves in quick motions, hauling in the dirt to cover the body.

She gives the ground a good pat before stepping back to admire her truly exhausting work.

She clears her throat and lets a sad smile bloom on her face.

"Here now lies June Birkstone. A truly wicked girl that pretty much everyone loved. The biggest bitch to have ever lived. I make this promise to you and only you, June. I will do everything in my mortal power to keep that fucker behind the door. He won't get out." Tears flow down her flushed cheeks. She lets them.

July kisses the tips of her fingers, planting them atop the freshly dug dirt, and then turning back to return the shovel and fix the lock to the tool shed.

# 31. Hello, Mother

She notices something odd as she moves through the many stalks of corn. They all instantly rot, drying to match the other fields surrounding the town.

Huh. It looks like His power is what kept it all alive for years. She must have pissed him off badly. Good. That *evil* deserves to wither in a supernatural prison for all eternity.

July doesn't stop in the manor to clean herself up. Instead, she makes her way through the old house and out to the front door and took a seat right on the porch.

Her body is slick with blood, yellow muck, and dirt. Her fingernails throb with various splinters and cuts. She looks like a mess.

Vivid flashes of tonight's events flicker in her mind until the sun rises. The recent memories warm her along with the early morning glow radiating from the sunrays. It's enough to act like an embrace.

When was the last time she was hugged? She can't seem to remember.

More hours pass by. Her body is sticky and caked with gross shit.

Birds croak their morning song. Grasshoppers flutter in the growing breeze. The sound of gravel being crushed beneath something fuels the dread within her.

July squares her shoulder at the sight of Abigail in the old truck getting closer to the manor. Well, she better come up with something believable to explain her sister's sudden disappearance.

Abigail parks the car and shoots her a quick smile. However, it melts into a frown. Then it becomes an expression of terror as she hurries out of the truck, not bothering to shut the driver's door while doing so.

She watches her mother clutching her ragged tassel lined purse. Her mouth is gaping at her. Jeez. There's no need to look like a breathless fish on her account.

"Why do you look like that? What happened? Where's your sister? I just knew she would pull something the moment I left." Her questions only give July a headache.

The girl shakes her head slowly. "June was running away with a boy she was seeing from another town. I accidentally found letters between them hidden in her vanity drawer. I hadn't mean to snoop…"

Really? That's the best she can come up with? Too late to try and shift the story now.

Her mother scoffs and crosses her arms urging for her to continue.

"She got so angry at me that she couldn't even pack anything. I chased her down the stairs and saw both the front and back door open. I had assumed she went through the corn and kept the front opened as a trick. Well, I assumed wrong and got lost for a good while in the woods. I tripped a few times on my way back. I'm so sorry." That last part isn't a lie.

July wishes it could have gone differently. But she wasn't given enough time to find any alternative than murdering her sister.

Abigail shakes her head and clicks her tongue in disappointment. This might be the first time the noise hasn't been directed at her. It only deepens the guilt that's starting to wallow in her belly.

"Did ya get a good look at the boy? Maybe the police can determine who he is based on his handwriting in the letters." Her mother nods her head and gets ready to go up the steps.

July's eyes go wide in panic. She jolts to a standing position. Her teeth grind against each other as her knees groan in pain.

She clears her throat. "No, I didn't get a look at him. It was dark and they had already lost me in the swamp. And I saw June stuff their letters inside her jacket. She refused to tell me where they were headed."

Damn. She should join the church theater with this performance.

Abigail huffs. Her eyes water. She lets her tears fall.

She doesn't blame her unease. It's good to be upset. It'd be cruel to tell her that June is in fact buried in the cornfield and won't ever leave Birkstone Manor.

Too bad she can't muster an ounce of all that spunk June had.

"Well, I'm going to inform the police anyways, so they know a teenager is on the loose with her estranged boyfriend." She pushes past July and heads into the manor.

July doesn't stop her. In fact, she's going to let her run this wild goose chase.

No more harm can be done.

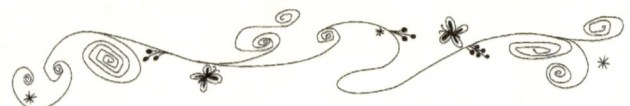

# 32. Aftermath

The following three days are slower than a slug trying to slither on the sidewalk in a fit of rain.

This is the first morning that Abigail has willingly got out of bed and put on a new change of clothes. It's also the first time July fixed breakfast. Not that it was ever hard to cook up some grits and put out the sugar and butter to accompany it.

They sit in silence. July picks at the lukewarm grits while her mother doesn't dare lift her spoon.

"We're moving back to Dallas to live with your grandparents." Abigail finally breaks the silence.

July drops her spoon in shock. It clatters against the dark blue porcelain bowl and unintentionally splatters some of the grits across the kitchen island.

She shakes her head. Her chest swells with panic. She can't leave Birkstone Manor.

She clears her throat and gives her best smile. Although it's more along the lines of a pained grimace.

"I'm not leaving Swamp Hill. My father left the house with me and June. Since she left that leaves it solely to me. I want to talk to your lawyer and put it in my name." She juts out her chin to appear more confident in this and herself.

The spare pair of glasses she found in her things still packed in a few boxes slid down her oily nose. She shoves it back up the bridge, scrunching her nose in discomfort.

As the saying goes, fake it till you make it.

Abigail nods slowly.

When the police arrived later after her mother came home, they told them that there was nothing to be done. The twins are of legal age. June can't be declared missing because July witnessed her leave on her own free will. That of course sent Abigail into a spiral.

"Okay. I'm going to pack what I want to take with me. You can have everything else." She mutters and gets off the stool. Leaving July alone in the kitchen.

July stands on the front porch. The setting sun graces her shoulders, warming her body and the bones that sometimes fail to keep her standing.

Her mother gives her a faint kiss upon the cheek before getting into the truck after tossing her few bags into the bed of it.

She still feels the woman's lips linger on her flesh. She'll treasure it for as long as she's able. There is no telling if Abigail plans to come back or not. Perhaps she shouldn't. Dead Fawn will be watching July's every move. That may include her mother too.

It takes tremendous strength to force a farewell smile on her face. She waves her hand in goodbye as her mother drives down the gravel road.

When she can no longer hear the roaring engine of the truck July collapses to her knees in a fit of sobs. She couldn't keep herself together a second longer. Her chest pulls in on itself like she's being slammed in a rollercoaster cart.

She feels like a different person. As if some part of her died the moment she plunged that knife into her sister's chest. There's an empty place within her heart.

Nothing can be done about it. No amount of glee or pride will fix it. She doesn't want it to be repaired. It's meant to be a constant reminder of what she lost and what she prevented from happening.

June may have been the bane of her existence, but she helped her build some thick inner walls.

She'll forever be damned if she refuses to use it for something worth fighting for. Such as keeping the people of Swamp Hill safe despite their uncertainty about her.

July forces herself to stop her tears. No more should be shed. What's done is done.

They've lived in that house for almost eight weeks, and she once hated the idea of going into the attic or basement. Hell, she's never been in the garage. And that's where she'll begin her exploration.

Instead of going out of the back door she makes way to the other side of the kitchen that leads to the garage.

No fear swells in her as she meets the darkness. She swallows that potential fright and uses her hands to glide against the nearest wall. Eventually, her fingers find the light switch.

Dim yellow light fills the garage. A genuine smile eases on her lips as she takes sight of the dusty old two door Jeep in the middle of the concrete floor.

Most of the garage is bare. She determines everything important had long since been stored in the tool shed. What does litter the walls are spare car parts and other things like that.

July finds the keys to the Jeep sitting perfectly on the handle.

She carefully wipes dust off the side of the door. It reveals a pleasant burgundy shade. Scratches hardly dot the surface. To her surprise, the interior is quite in tack. This wasn't mentioned in their father's will.

For a moment, she considers calling dibs on it. But then she remembers she is the lone Birkstone occupying the manor. Everything in this place is now or will be soon all hers legally.

She takes this as the first good sign of living in this fucked up town.

With the first turn of the keys the engine comes to life with a sputtering cry.

Yes. It seems the gloomy tides are shifting for the better.

# 33. A New Life

July and June never walked across the stage at their early graduation along with a few others in their senior class. That fact should make her feel sad and guilty she didn't live up to her personal goals. None of her college applications were sent out. She hadn't made any friends to spend one last epic summer with.

Well, that's no serious matter.

She knew the moment she promised her sister's dead corpse to keep *evil* at bay that any chance at college or a real life was erased. There wouldn't be a need to consume herself with mountains of homework and invest in research papers.

This is much more important.

She makes the choice to head into town after spending a few days cleaning the manor and locking doors that don't ever need to be opened again.

July boarded up the room she shared with her sister and cleaned the master bedroom on the bottom floor. Her mother decided not to use it when they first moved in. She walked inside the room and saw all the cobwebs and layers of dust covering various surfaces.

The old Jeep drives smoothly. The brakes don't squeal as she parks in the parking lot in the middle of town. The steering wheel feels oddly perfect under her frail boney hands.

A few people give her curious glares. Wondering where her mother and sister are perhaps. She masks the truth with a smile as she hops out of the Jeep while being careful of her knees. They're black and purple with major bruises. She's got her hands wrapped as well with plenty of healing ointment and bandages.

July looks like a mummy. But she doesn't give a shit about the odd looks aimed at her as she walks down the sidewalk with her chin held high and shoulders squared.

However, she can sense Dead Fawn in the small crowds that linger in various shops, examining trinkets and choosing which candies to bring home to their crying children.

None make a move to approach her. Maybe their leader ordered them not to. That's good for them. She won't hesitate to lash out. The people of this town know more than they ever led on about the manor and purple door. It'd be a shame if they arrested their only source of protection for public retaliation.

She figures the police would look the other way, allowing her to do some dirty work and keep Him locked away. Only time will tell.

No one is in the bookstore when she casually struts inside. The owner is leaning over the front counter making clicking noises on the register, her brows furrowed in concentration.

The sound of the front door's bell interrupts her. She looks upon July as if suddenly seeing a ghost.

"July? Thank the Gods above us. You're alive! I was so worried." The older woman hurries around the counter to embrace her.

She can't remember if this woman has ever truly spoken to her. But the comfort she offers is much appreciated.

After a long moment July pulls back with raised brows, wondering what's this is about. The reason isn't so obvious to her. Perhaps she has heard of her stopping Dead Fawn.

"W-What are you talking about?" July asks to try not to sound so smug about it. She had a feeling this woman knew things. She seemed to be good friends with Ms. Tibbs.

The woman takes her shoulders gently. Her stern gaze is rather piercing. She gulps down the nervous belch that rises in her throat.

"I and a few others have been watching you. It was I who gave the book to Ms. Tibbs so that she could invest it in you. But now I can see that she also played a part in this small powerful victory. I just know she would have been proud." She watches the woman's eyes glisten. A sorrowful haze engulfing them at the mention of Ms. Tibbs.

Guilt seeps into her gut, tearing at her inner walls. It's mocking her. Telling her she could have saved the librarian if she truly wanted to. And yet it's her heart that says there was nothing she could have done. The woman's fate wasn't in her hands to begin with.

Shit. Even that sounds horrible. A thought that should have never crossed her mind.

July is going to use it nonetheless as fuel to further motivate her cause.

"I…umm… I'm staying in town to y'know… Make sure He doesn't get out." She keeps her voice low, leaning close to whisper.

There may not be anyone besides them in the store but that doesn't stop her from being quiet about it. It doesn't hurt to keep calm. This soft tone is what's keeping her bubbling asthma attack at bay. Her sinuses are starting to itch. She feels a sneeze coming on.

The woman nods her head frantically, tears swelling in her eyes. However, the look of despair she had earlier now morphs into an expression of relief.

"What can I do for you?" The woman asks.

Before opening her mouth to answer she peers at the nametag pinned to the woman.

July clears her throat and does her best to smile. Though, it looks more like a grimace than anything else. "I'd like a job, Miss Dunnly. If you have an opening that is."

The bookstore owner, Miss Dunnly, offers her a small smile that is filled with an emotion she can't determine. It may be pity or sadness. She doesn't linger on the detail long enough to figure it out.

"Yes. Of course. Letting you work here is the least I can do in thanks for your bravery. Let me show you around the store." She pulls July into a bone crushing hug once again.

This time she wraps her arms firmly around Miss Dunnly, soaking in the warmth and support she didn't know she craved.

Before heading out of town to venture into the piney woods to reach Birkstone Manor, July stops at a hardware store to get a few supplies.

She had her entire savings stashed where June and their mother couldn't find it. Plus, their father also left them a large sum. According to the lawyer who called her this morning on the landline, since June left without officially graduating, her portion goes to July.

Now how's that for a well-earned commission? There is plenty to live on for many years to come.

A few stray glances stay on her for the most part while in the store. She ignores them as she reaches for a few bundles of rope and about six yards of barbed wire fence. She'll need to purchase more of them eventually.

July paid for those and the rest of the many supplies she plans to regularly replenish such as hooks, bear traps, and mace.

It is rather satisfying dumping everything out of the brown paper bags and onto the kitchen island after she gets back home.

She takes a deep breath and searches through many of the kitchen drawers for a note pad and pen. Her mind swells with a system that will improve this method of keeping Him away.

Once she does, July takes inventory of her supplies and what their various uses will be. She logs the amount per tool and weapon. Already coming up with ways to enforce Birkstone Manor.

July plans to booby-trap the entire estate and the land with it. It's the only way to keep unwanted Dead Fawn followers out and away from the purple door. They will learn that even though she's somewhat broke, July will kick ass.

She smiles down at the many bundles of rope, a dozen rolls of duct tape, and other various items that will certainly come in handy.

# 34. This Is The End?

It's late in the month of June. Winter has long gone and left a giant hole in its wake. Spring blew past wonderfully with breezes filled with satisfaction. Now the hard part is trying not to melt into a puddle due to this tragic summer heat.

Texas can be brutal. That includes the weather and its people. Only one of them has she barely begun to manage.

July stands in front of the large pot currently bubbling over the stove.

She shoves her recently chopped hair behind her ears. It feels good to no longer have the strands wrap around her neck and stick to her with sweat. The sensation it brought on would send shivers down her spine, causing her to give an occasional shiver.

The spices she tosses into the black pot of cooking chili impregnate the air. Birkstone Manor smells pleasant and looks incredible as the setting sun sinks behind the bare field surrounding it.

It's burning orange rays seep through the kitchen, causing her hair to glow.

A long time ago she decided to open all the windows of the rooms that she keeps unlocked. It proved to be rather uplifting. Trapping herself in darkness didn't offer anything meaningful.

It only brought on paranoia. She doesn't want to live a life filled with fear and having to constantly look over her shoulder. Good thing she's found ways to help with that and still keep a close watch on the door.

She uses a wood spoon to stir her dinner. The popping deep red bubbles that burst with tongue-watering flavors echo over the faint music playing from the jukebox behind her on the island. She was elated that it still worked after finding it in the tool shed a few weeks ago.

July glances down at her hands. Faint scars litter her fingers. Just old memories of what happened this past winter. No need to dwell on it longer than she needs to.

Noting the small glass mug containing iced sweet tea sitting on the counter brings a smile to her face. It's a simple pleasure like this that makes life worth something.

The tea is nice and tasty as it slides over her tongue and into the back of her throat. Her upper lip is wet with the remainders of her drink. She uses the back of her hand to wipe it off.

A timer goes off next to her to her left of the stove. She jolts in surprise. Her small laughter shaking her shoulders as she fetches mitts to reveal fresh cornbread from the hot oven.

It doesn't take long to make her a bowl of chili with the side cornbread and a newly replenished tea. The perfect dinner. She plans to have a can of Dr. Pepper for dessert while on the phone with Abigail. They call each other once a week. July still hasn't come clean about June's death. She isn't ever going it.

Her stomach gurgles just as she dips her spoon into the meal. But it clatters out of her hand as a blaring alarm fills the kitchen. Mother fucker.

July takes a deep breath, stilling her racing heart to relax.

She's been waiting for this moment for months. To say that she is prepared is an understatement. This should be a piece of cake, honestly. Only if she can pull this off without revenge getting in the way of the one true motive. Keeping Him at bay and not letting Dead Fawn get their way.

She calmly gets up to put a paper towel over her still steaming bowl of chili to keep it warm. She then marches into the garage and fetches an old shotgun someone in town is renting to her. People don't mess around when it comes to their guns. If she even scratches this hefty tool, then she'll be forced to pay extra.

July is saving up to someday soon buy her own small arsenal. But for right now she's opting to rent.

By the sound of this alarm, it seems that someone has gotten themselves in a bear trap along the south border of the property. They better hope they can get out of it before July reaches them.

She doesn't bother shutting the back door as she quickly steps down the porch steps.

There's still enough sunlight to see out in the distance.

The culprit managed to drag his ruined leg still stuck in the trap all the way to the door. His sweaty face and dirty clothes do nothing to mask the angry haze in his eyes.

"We will release Him. His time shall come!" The flushed man hollers, aiming to ruffle her composure.

July bends her neck to the left. *POP!* Then to the right. *CRACKK!*

She aims the shotgun at him. "Yeah? Well, you can personally tell Him to go fuck Himself."

Her finger squeezes the trigger. The bullet hits him in the skull right between his eyes. His body goes limp and collapses to the ground. She takes a few steps towards it, still cautious in case somehow *evil* finds the strength to bring the body back to life.

Reports of a few teenagers sleepwalking outside of their houses have been stirring in town. They're planning something. Preparing for the next blue moon. Well, He won't be powerful enough to fully possess someone else for a very long time.

She's carved runes into the door that symbolize entrapment as well as pays a priest from out of town to come and bless the field. Whatever it takes to dampen Him.

There's a strange irony about how this straggler landed. His arms and legs are perfectly aligned to form an upside down cross. An attempt to sway her confidence.

*Yeah, fuck you too.*

July huffs in satisfaction before turning around and heading back inside the manor to finally enjoy her chili that she spent half the day making. Her stomach growls at the thought of adding hot sauce to it.

Everything is going swell. No need to be hasty and waste the perfect summer meal. She'll bury the body deep in the woods later along with the rest of her secrets.

# Epilogue

Over the following years, July Birkstone learned to defend the manor she's grown to love and keep Dead Fawn from getting to Him. Her time alone in almost total self-isolation proved useful and rather uneventful. There had only been three deaths caused by her hand.

She likes to call it her streak of good luck.

The older boy who killed Ms. Tibbs in spite of her actions almost seventy years ago came around Birkstone Manor every Friday, taunting her with ominous threats and teasing. She learned his name to be Tanner Forger after demanding it from him while shooting an arrow in his foot.

Her theory of the leader position being passed down to each male generation had also been correct.

He would tell her the same thing. "One day He will return."

If not that then it'd be, "Live a pleasant life while you can, little girl."

Despite their aging he'd continue with the pathetic nick-name.

July formed the habit of showing off her shot gun in answer. All he'd do was smile and shake his head, already had he faced her wrath. His once black hair gained many gray strands, foiling his once menacing presence.

But one day during the last five years a younger man had revealed himself. He told July he'd been the grandson of Tanner. Let's just say she gave him a warning shot and told him to get the fuck off her property. This time it had been a bullet to hit him in the foot. He fled with his tail pinned between his legs.

Old habits sure die fucking hard.

Every once in a while, a few Dead Followers take a turn trying to evade the various trip wires and hundreds of hidden bear traps within the corn field.

None have gotten close enough to the purple door. Most grew scared and would flee before July got the chance to get her shotgun or crossbow.

She's led a peaceful routine that hardly anything disrupts. And yet today feels a little different.

July tossed and turned all night. Sleep would not welcome her no matter how much she begged for it. Her already aching bones groaned as she slipped out of her sheets during the early morning.

The much older woman takes her time in making her coffee. She shovels three spoons of sugar into the steaming mug along with caramel flavored creamer. A nifty way to spruce up her favorite drink.

After taking a long sip, letting the creamy drink warm her throat, she hopes her unsettled feeling must get better.

She pulls her frilly housecoat around her waist to shield against the early winter cold.

The final signs of fall have long since passed. The trees have shed their leaves, baring their branches for birds who continue to migrate south. A heavy winter is upon this dreary town. There's hardly anyone left in Swamp Hill other than her, a few locals, and the deadly cult.

Most left due to the lack of rain and brutal season that never felt quite right. July never blamed them for leaving. It gave her more freedom to act as crazy as she wanted to warn the followers of Him. That included chasing them through town in her Jeep she wrapped with bared wire and spikes on the tires.

With a heavy sigh, July carefully walks out onto the back porch. A gentle breeze tinged with cold seeps into her bones. She welcomes the pleasant touch with a soft smile as she ventures to the little table and rocking chair she bought two decades ago.

A simple piece of furniture that offers comfort even during her darkest moments.

However, after she settles and takes sight of the once bare field her heart sinks. She stutters to her feet, gasping in shock.

This can't be! She's been so damn careful. Why didn't any of the alarms go off?

July rushes to the porch rails, her fingers gripping the iron bars for dear life, afraid that if she lets go that she'll disappear.

Blood. So much blood stains the ground before the door that continues to drift open and close due to the wind.

She sees the dead body of a teenager with her precious throat slashed lying before it as well.

July brings a shaky hand covered in age spots to shield her gaping mouth. Tears sting her eyes.

They had done it. She missed the blue moon. This can't be possible. July had this marked on a calendar. There were no recent signs of possible possession within the town. What went wrong?

Knowing that she couldn't have prevented this doesn't ease the sudden pain in her chest. Her hiss flutters in the wind as she aggressively leans onto the rail. A striking thump in her heart causes July to inhale deeply. For a moment she breaks into a fit of coughs.

She clutches her chest, twisting the front of her nightgown. Once she regains her composure July notes the fresh blood now slathered on her palm. Damn. Another thing she needs to worry about.

Returning her sight on the unlocked purple door has tears slipping from her hazy brown eyes.

"God, help us all." She mutters. It's answered by a dark chuckle behind her. The sound is the opposite of warm and inviting. And yet she recognizes it perfectly.

It's been pushing into her mind for such a long time. Never letting her forget what she did to June, her poor sister who fell victim to Him. Blaming her for *evil's* own greed and hunger for control and chaos.

She goes stiff as a plank when a heavy warm breath caresses the back of her neck. July tugs at the bottom of her silver braid, wishing she had died in her sleep during the night.

Whatever security she forced herself to feel is nowhere to be found. It was just an illusion she's only just now seeing through.

"Yer here to collect me, aren't ya?" Her voice is no more than a croak from all the smoking she's done.

A bad habit she picked up to spite her mother who used to blame her for June's disappearance. She failed to correct her mother on the subject. Instead, she chose to punish herself for years and years.

He answers by laying a hand on her right shoulder. She dares to take a look at it. Her eyes grow large as she quickly studies the way His pitch-black fingers and sharp nails dig into her housecoat. The sharp pain of it is nothing compared to the fear lacing her guts.

She guesses that His twisted horns look the same as they did when He was a mere shadow in search of a way out.

Nothing else is said. July feels a final quick pain in her chest and her vision turns milky white. She prays that it's death on the other end that will somehow relieve her of *evil*.

Airs fills her lungs unexpectedly.

July thrusts upward with a chilling inhale that rattles her body. Her suddenly young body that is. Huh? That's not right.

She peers at herself and finds her very bare limbs and arms to be free of wrinkles and age spots. Damnit. She's eighteen again. Where the fuck did He bring her?

She sits in a large pool of something dark- most likely blood- in an open plane of nothingness. The land is black with rot and burnt from fire that long ago ran wild it seems. It's speckled with sparse trees that lean in the worst angles. Dark red and silver clouds contain thunder and lightning in this ever-brewing nasty green sky. Even the wind is hot and swirls her loose hair like twine.

This must be the place June said she'd always end up. Well, how original on His part. As if she hasn't thought of the alternative to this like Heaven.

The second she returns to look upon herself once again, she finds a total of six beings standing before her. All of them are extremely muscular naked men that have truly terrifying goat heads. Every inch of their oily red skin is covered with brutal scars and open wounds that produce a nasty purple sludge. Their mouths are filled with sharp teeth. The drool that leaks off their hanging tongues is translucent red that reflects the surroundings like glass.

Jeez, there's so much blood that she can smell the stale iron stench from here.

She covers herself up. It does no good. They don't care for her bare body. Only the need to torment runs through their veins. She can see their thirst for it in their heated eyes.

And of course, *evil* knows exactly how to do so because her sister may have been the vessel to channel His power into, but she was never the true target. No. It was July this whole time. She was just too stupid to see Him enjoying the chase.

What an idiot she turned out to be. No wonder none of Dead Fawn tried anything against her. They were waiting for *evil* to get to her first.

When the closest goat-headed being reaches her and sinks his ever-growing claws into her leg she screams.

This is the hell He promised her. This is fucking hell.

# Bonus Material

# Bonus Chapter

The man's harsh staggered breathing keeps him company in the early morning darkness as he rushes out of the kitchen and into the living room. He doesn't dare take a glance over his shoulder to peer at the creature, the thing that the *evil* summoned for its bidding.

His father warned him of the dark voice behind the door before he passed tragically in a spontaneous drought fire in the cornfield. He should have stayed away like he begged him to.

It continues to torture him with its never-ending wails. A sickening noise that sounds so lifeless…deafening, even.

At first, the tormenting cries would cause an ache to appear in the front of his skull. But now it's everywhere like a battering ram that encourages echoing throbs to jolt down his neck and travel throughout his spine.

And to make it worse its looming shadow emits such coldness that everything it passes seems to frost over. A chill comes from it so bizarrely that you'd think it freezes the body and soul. He can imagine it's just a tad bit of power that *evil* can create.

He rather not see any more of it.

Looking at this disgusting creature is enough to make him want to vomit the eggs and bacon he had for supper just a few hours ago.

He trips over a flipped rug corner and tumbles onto his knees with a sickening thud. His bones and joints creak, sending a thrilling shock up his thigh and tailbone.

"Fuck." The man groans in distaste. A word he never uses because it always feels bitter on his tongue afterward. It was his grandfather's favorite to use. Maybe he is with him right now in spirit.

However, a dark chuckle behind him that seems muffled erases the grimace from his face, turning it into a deep frown. Fuck.

He takes a precious moment to shove a wave of dark blonde hair off his forehead. He had been meaning to get it cut. It keeps getting into his eyes, one brown and the other blue. Nervous sweat drips down the sides of his face. A drop trickles down into his left eye. It burns like hell, but he forces himself to get up off his ass and kneel before the creature. A truly pathetic move, but what else is he to do?

There are no more chances to get away.

This is it.

The breaths in his lungs quake. "P-Please. Don't hurt m-me."

Damn, it sure does hurt his chest to sound so pitiful. He's never like this. It's always been in his best interest to appear the least bit interesting.

It was safer for them that way.

How tragic. He'll never even get a chance to meet-

*"Hmm. Beg me some more. I like the taste of your fear."* A strangled voice answers him. And yet it does little to match the face of a twelve-year-old boy that stands in front of him.

The sweat in his eyes gets more intense, blurring his vision more than he hoped for. At least he won't look the damn thing in the eye before it kills him. That's better than nothing.

At first, he fails to respond. Beads of the salty substance trails down his spine, seeping into the top of his dark brown work slacks. He never did change out of his office clothes before making supper. Good thing he won't die in his Sponge Bob pjs no grown man should wear.

"Ain't gonna happen. I'm done being like yer lil bitch. Ya feel me?" Anger seeps into his words. That natural Southern twang everyone born in Texas has flutters in the back of his throat. And his just woke the fuck up to pick a fight. No reason to play nice.

From what he can make out, the deranged boy who is no longer human cracks his neck, preparing for something more.

In a quick flash, the hot breath of the creature-boy that *evil* commands wafts over his heated skin. It's about ninety degrees outside and he's sweating buckets despite it being November.

That's just Texas's luck he guesses.

*"Don't give yourself the satisfaction of taunting me. You are just a host, a being meant to be taken over by me and all that I am. You weren't the first I tried to take, and you surely won't be the last. The time will come, and I will be free. Too bad you won't be around to see that day."* No longer is the man smiling. In fact, his eyes now leak tears.

They stream down his face. His cheeks and neck unwillingly welcome an aggressive flush.

His stomach turns and practically pushes his half-digested supper up his throat. He swallows it out of whatever pride he has left.

The man gulps down his sudden nerves before puffing his chest. He's not going down without a fight. He smiles, hoping the oddly timed gesture will distract the creature from noticing him retrieve the switch blade hidden in his back pant pocket.

"You won't ever get out. The forces of *evil* will never win." In this moment he feels like the powerful one. But it's an illusion not meant to be permanent.

However, when he finally catches a better glimpse of the boy— Mr. Ben's youngest son from down the road— that quick confidence melts away like it was never anything other than a speck of dirt.

It grins at him. *"Well, thank you for the fortune. Time's up."*

With a quick hand, the creature slashes the man's throat with the very switch blade he momentarily held in his hands.

A gruesome rumble of thunder shoots through the sky. Bright purple lightening slashes within the murky gray clouds outside the massive manor. The flickering lights around the living room reveal the dead body of its owner, his fresh dark blood staining the carpet.

The boy who was once taken over by *evil* collapses soon after, a cloud of smoke lifting out of his gaping mouth.

# Another Bonus
# Chapter

She can hear it. That voice that hasn't stopped calling out to her since she and her stupid failure of a twin got here. But why can't July hear it like her? She must be more broken than June had originally thought.

It's cold tonight. The heater hasn't been working very well lately. Her mom said the repair man would be out later in the week. Well, it's later in the fucking week and no one has showed up yet.

Honestly, her mom is a total idiot about certain things. She's so pliable when it comes to getting stuff June wants. That woman is wrapped around her finger whether July approves or not. Of course, that doesn't matter either.

Who gives a fuck about July?

So, while the voice scratches the inside of her already thought-filled mind her toes are freezing. It's like an icebox in this room. If the temperature gets any lower, then she'll start looking for frost lining the walls.

June should steal some of July's blankets next time. The girl won't dare fight her for them back. She trained her well in that regard.

After flipping to her other side, she clenches her eyes tight, hoping it will go away.

But it doesn't. It keeps poking at her, testing certain points to see where she's most vulnerable. What the fuck is that?

And then it abruptly pulls back. There's an echoing emptiness in her chest. Almost like she misses its constant badgering.

June gives a heavy sigh and adjusts to where she lays on her back. That's the only sound filling the room. An earie silence engulfs the air. She can't even hear the chirps from crickets or caws from the ravens outside. Her fingers grip her sheets tight, knuckles blanching white from her hold.

A rush of heat collapses over her. It produces a sudden compulsion for her to jolt out of bed and strip her clothes off.

It's so hot.

She's boiling.

Sweat drips down the valley of her breasts, soaking her night clothes. They cling to her body like a second skin.

Once the cold air hits her searing skin she gives a groan of relief. With startled eyes she peers at July, worried she woke the poor girl. She so doesn't want to hear any of her nagging.

Instead, she finds her sister's breath forming small clouds before her trembling lips.

June leans forward as she wipes her forehead with the back of her hand. Are July's lips tinged blue or is she seeing things?

There's no way it's that cold in here while she's pouring with sweat. She really needs a shower.

Just as she moves to her pretty dresser lined with all her perfumes something wicked in her chest seizes her to a stop. She can't seem to move her arms to sift through the first drawer and fetch a new fresh pair of pajamas and underwear.

Invisible ropes twist around her limbs. Inhibiting her from moving at all. It sparks panic in her. Nerves eat at her guts, swimming in her fear like little maggots she once found in an apple at breakfast last week at school.

She attempts to shriek as something wicked slides over her shoulders and down her back. It feels like a vine littered with thorns. They scratch her skin, marring her flesh with cuts.

A flash of moonlight slips through the window and illuminates the weeds and vines swarming her side of the room. Just like before. And when July manages to wake her again before the door not remembering how she got there she'll pull them out of the floor and wall. Her sister thinks she has no idea she does this. But it's hard not to recognize signs of missing memories and clear confusion.

And yet this night is different. She always goes blank after trying to head to the shower down the dark hall. Her mind clears of all thought, and she wakes up naked and freezing in the field.

Why can't she go back to sleep like before? What's going to happen now that she's fully awake but lacking control over her own body? This fucking blows. Worse than running out of her favorite lip gloss.

The questions matter not as a strange caress guides her limbs to move. No matter how hard she tries June fails to cover herself. She'd much rather be beneath a hot football player on full display. Certainly not this. This is fucking humiliating.

She can't get a good look at her sister before she's out of their room and down the stairs. Her head continues to look forward. Her sight is attached to what's in front of her.

This isn't like the other times at all. She dreads finding out why.

June keeps going through the living room and out of the back door within the kitchen.

The outside cold fails to prick her flesh, doing what it can to penetrate the heat engulfing her. She's a boiling pot of freshly steeping tea that doesn't want to cool off.

Nothing looks out of the ordinary as she's compelled to take the porch steps. The marble is smooth beneath her feet. No matter that her body is so incredibly warm she can still feel a slight breeze on her bare ass.

At least she can briefly roll her eyes.

Stalks of corn gently lean around her to caress every inch of her exposed skin. It's like they have a mind of their own or are being controlled.

A faint whimper is trapped behind her closed mouth. Thirteen people of all ages are circled around the purple door that's surrounded by dozens of blazing candles. Oh, she's so fucked.

One with long black hair steps forth a wicked grin. Yet he isn't eyeing her like a piece of precious candy. Most men would. Before coming to this horrid little town, she had a body like a goddess. Lately she can feel herself slacking.

She'll fix that if she somehow can wake herself of this nightmare.

He says a sputter of words in a language she can't comprehend.

Him and the others take a deep bow and turn around. She watches them walk into the corn and disappear. Leaving the guy a little older than her to grip her by the shoulder in an oddly careful hold to bring her closer to the door.

June desperately screams in her mind to be let go. Afraid he might get a crazy idea to have his way with her. And yet his eyes don't have that familiar haze clouding them like most older men who like her a little too much. Instead, his dark eyes are filled with something else. It looks more sinister.

She's so fucked.

"Welcome to the cause, June Birkstone. You've been chosen by Him to help break free the lock on His prison. Try not to fuck it up for us." He says with a smile and gestures to the door that's suddenly glowing.

She struggles to cry out. It's no use. All thoughts of escape flee her mind as she watches a dark cloud of purple and yellow smoke snake out from behind the door to gather before her.

Tears leak down her face. She no longer cares about her naked self. It seems so insignificant to what may be in store for her. And this fucking heat flash is killing her, now making its way through her blood and muscles. It feels like she's going to melt into a nasty puddle of meat slush.

The multicolored smoke forms into a shape. One that she never thought to be real. She recalls seeing it out the corner of her eyes in the hallways at school and sometimes in the manor.

She now knows the voice belongs to it. To Him.

Her lips wobble as an entirely pitch-black clawed hand takes hold of both of hers to raise them up, palms facing the dark blue sky.

That voice again fills her mind. This time she can't stop herself from hearing it.

*"I've waited many years to meet you, July Birkstone. You are exactly what I call for. Now, I can finally get rid of this pathetic door keeping me here. Trust me when I say you will be greatly rewarded for your participation. Please, you must enjoy this. It's the rarest of honors."* His voice is deep as a gurgling sound from an erupting volcano. It scratches her mind enough to make her cringe.

She wants to shout how delusional He sounds but can't get her mouth to move to do so. Nothing is working. Fear lingers in her bones, fueling this thing.

As she takes in the sight of his tragically twisted horns her heart squeezes. She doesn't want to die. Not in the way he plans. It's not fair.

She must go to that fucking dance!

More vines rise from the ground, coiling around her legs and eventually her arms. Their thorns leak something fiercely resembling blood. A gag makes its way to her throat.

She can feel Him smile down at her. His dark chuckles vibrate her body. This is so not happening.

Without meaning to, her mouth drops open. June can't stop herself from tiling her head backward.

A different waft of smoke seeps out of the crack in the door. It glows yellow and is flickers with strange sparkles. It electrifies the air, sending jolts into the tips of her fingers.

He leans into her more. God, she can smell his breath. It's a mixture of decay and something along the lines of mint. The worst toothpaste scent known to man.

*"June, there is no need to beg for mercy when I am your new God. Now, taste what the future has to offer you."* The moment He snaps His fingers the brilliant-colored smoke dives into her mouth and the back of her throat.

She jerks and the vines tighten themselves around her, drawing blood from newly opening wounds in her skin. There's nothing she can do. June feels the darkness wrapping around her organs one at a time. It sinks its teeth into her. It won't ever let go. He won't ever release her from His hold.

June is herself until the second it reaches her heart. Her mind then is filled with flashes of darkness and chaos. None is what she wants. She cries against her restraints as an image of July's mutilated body caused by her hands flash.

Oh, how cruel she has been to that girl. And for what? The fun of it?

Just as quickly as His will invades June it changes her entirely. Her mind is void. Entirely empty and waiting.

No childhood memories or thoughts of recent and upcoming events are there.

It's a blank canvas that He now has complete control of.

She is his to wield in the battle against His foes. The frail July Birkstone won't be able to put an end to Him.

# Acknowledgements

First of all, thank you everyone for even picking up this book. It means a lot that you showed interest in my writing. I worked really hard on this novel and hope you enjoy every bit of it.

Secondly, thank you to the folks who have been following me along my writing career since perhaps *The Mush* and *Save Our King*. It is so great to feel your support and know that y'all have continued to enjoy what I create. This of course relates to ARC readers of this book and the others. Trust me when I say that there is more to come and it will be epic.

Lastly, thank you to family and friends who have been there to support me. I couldn't have kept my writing going without y'all.

# About the author

Harlie has been a passionate writer for years. She enjoys fantasy romance and horror novels the most. Her favorite books of all time are *The Hobbit* and *Interview With The Vampire*. When she isn't writing, Harlie can be found rewatching her favorite TV shows and movies or spending time with friends and family. This is her second novel in the horror genre and she hopes to one day be a full-time writer. She lives with her family and many pets.